The Gentle Art of Making Enemies

Volume I

Cover art and illustration by Walter Sablotny III

Copyright © 2012 Walter Sablotny III

ISBN: 0615879470

ISBN-13: 978- 0615879475 (paledark Books)

For Patrick Beifuss and Jim House,
who were there in the beginning;
Kevin Gruzewski, who was there at the end;
and my brother Joe, who's been there the whole time.

1997

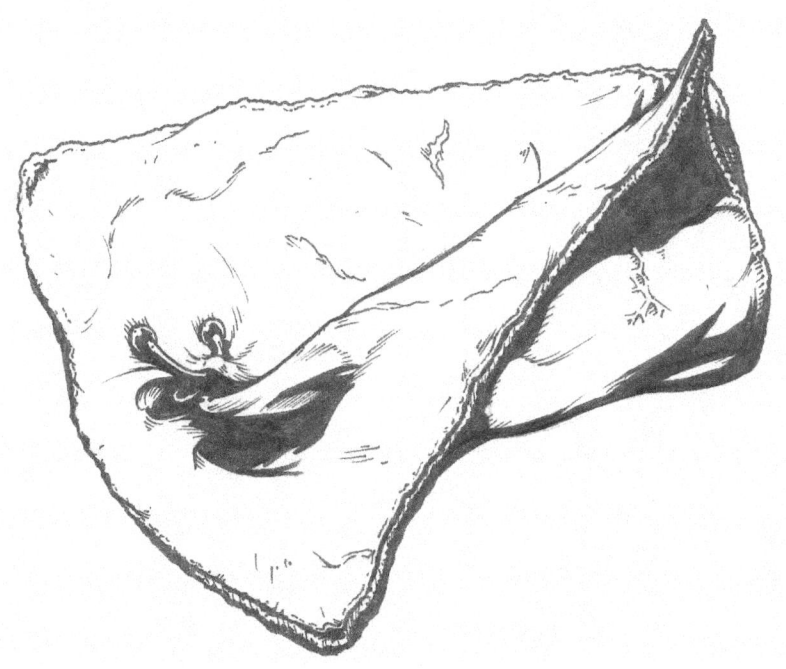

Kevin Mellor

1

Pete

The waitress was taking forever to get our orders, which is not a good idea when Dave is in your section. There's not much to do in a restaurant but order food and eat it, and Dave gets a little out of hand when he's bored. He's all about food, so if you can keep him thinking about it or shoving it into his mouth with both hands, things will usually go okay. But we didn't eat at the same restaurants often enough for waitresses to recognize us, with the turnover rate in the food service industry as high as it is, so there's no way a waitress can possibly know what kind of trouble Dave can be. It's all very confusing. We rarely got the same waitress twice. I think Lucas planned it that way.

We'd been waiting for twenty minutes. Dave had already slurped down everybody's ice water and Lucas had gone through a cigarette and a half. I was spinning coins, which is pointless but mildly amusing nonetheless. There was something about the way they looked when you really got them going, like perfect balls, that pleased me. And I found that staring at them as they changed from little balls of illusion to flat pieces of crap clattering on a tabletop had a strange sort of soothing effect, which is always a good trick to have in your bag.

It was a little after 9:00, so the restaurant was pretty dead. It was one of those places that wants to be a cross between a Denny's and some upscale place and doesn't really cut it either way. The only people in the smoking section were the three of us, and a frat rat and two soratory bitches at the table across the aisle from us. They'd given us dirty looks as soon as we sat down and then went into their privileged-rich-kid routine, talking about stuff louder than they needed to because they get a little thrill out of thinking you're interested in their lives and love to act offended if it looks like you're listening. I personally blame this on MTV, which spends half of its programming time showing melodramatic frat and soratory kids crying about stupid shit. Then again, for all I know, frat and soratory kids may have always acted like this, and some TV asshole finally figuring out how to make a profit on it is only a recent development.

And for the record, I know that *soratory* is not an actual word. It was just one of those things one of us came up with that made the other guys laugh, and it stuck. Like me calling Lucas *cunt'ry* instead of country, and Lucas saying *fuck-all*. As in "We need to find some beer, cause we got fuck-all to do tonight."

I was watching a penny with a patch of turquoise tarnish on it, admiring the spot in the middle of the ball, when out of the corner of my eye I saw one of the soratory bitches, the hotter one, slide out of her booth and walk past our table.

"That girl just walked into the bathroom with a cell phone," Dave said.

"Good," I said.

Dave stuck his hand up by his ear, pinky and thumb out, the universal I'm-pretending-to-be-on-the-phone gesture. "She's sitting on the pot—'Hello, Jen? It's me, Jen. I...' *PTHHBBB!*"

6

Yeah, I know, pretty crude, but it made me laugh. Even the corner of Lucas' mouth looked like it was smiling. It may not sound like much, but for Lucas that's pretty good. I don't think he ever learned how to smile with both sides of his mouth at the same time.

The boyfriend guy at their table glared at Dave. "You think you're fucking funny?"

"Beg your pardon?" Dave said.

"You think you're fucking funny, making fun of her?"

"Well... yeah?" Dave nodded. "Why else would I do it?"

This was apparently not the answer Boyfriend Guy was looking for. "Fuck you," he said.

"Don't get your panties all in a bunch over it," Dave told him. "I'm sorry, alright? Sometimes I forget that words can hit as hard as a fist."

"Fuck you," Boyfriend Guy said.

If you can't give him credit for originality, you might give him points for being able to remember something long enough to say it two times in a row. Of course, he was wearing a frat t-shirt, so he gets no points for anything.

I looked at Lucas, but he was giving a large rubber plant a thousand-yard stare and chewing the inside of his bottom lip, which means he's deep in thought about something. "This could get ugly," I said under my breath.

"Listen jagload," Dave was telling Boyfriend Guy. "I'm trying to apologize."

Phone Girl came back from the bathroom. She had a nice rack. Really nice. She was wearing one of those white spaghetti-strap tank tops and some kind of strapless bra that kept you from seeing nipple but held the rest of her up and out so much that it didn't really take away from the breast-viewing experience as a whole.

"What's going on?" she said.

"This asshole was making fun of your phone," Boyfriend Guy said. He didn't look at her. He was staring at Dave, trying to psyche him out.

"I am *sooooo* fucking sorry lady," Dave said. He stole Lucas' cigarette off the lip of the ashtray and started smoking it. Lucas lit another one.

"You don't sound sorry," Boyfriend Guy said.

"Why would you make fun of my phone?" the Phone Girl said. I think she was trying to go for the whole disgusted-and-hurt-but-still-cute thing, but she just sounded like a whiny bitch with great tits.

"You took it to the bathroom!" Dave said. "If that's not good comedy, I don't know what is."

"Don't you fucking swear in front of her!" Boyfriend Guy yelled back. If he understood the concept of irony, which I doubt, he had apparently decided not to let it hold him back in life.

Somebody had to do something, and since Lucas is never going to stop any kind of fight, and I was hungry and actually wanted to eat at least half a meal before being kicked out, it would have to be me.

"You have a cell phone," I said to Phone Girl.

"Yes."

"In this restaurant."

"*Yes.*"

The other blonde girl at their table, who's tits weren't as big and who was wearing too much makeup to try and replace what nature had shorted her on, decided it was time to throw her two cents in. "Katie, why are you even talking to these losers? They're *dirty*."

Now that's just unfair. I'm very, very clean. Lucas showers at least once a day, although he does tend to look dirty because he dresses like a lumberjack-turned-wino. Dave is dirty. He showers like once every two weeks, so his hair and skin are really oily and his clothes get all soft and rumpled. But he wears deodorant and cologne and brushes his teeth at least 6 times a day, so it's not like he gives off a foul odor of some sort. He just looks wet all the time.

"You have a cell phone," I said, trying to get back on track. "In this restaurant. To make and receive phone calls."

"*Yes!*" Phone Girl said. She held up her hand and waved the phone at me. To her credit, she refrained from any "nyah nyah nyah" sounds, although I could tell it was killing her. "What the fuck is your *problem?*"

Cell phones are just stupid. People think their lives are so important that they can't be out of contact with anybody for an hour without risking the collapse of society as we know it. Did you ever listen to the conversations people have on cell phones? They have to tell everybody where they are, what they're doing there, what time they'll be leaving, and what they're doing later. Having a cell phone is basically like paying a bunch of money every month so that everyone you know can treat you like your mom did when you were thirteen.

I might have tried to explain this to Phone Girl--not that it would have done any good, I'm sure--but I didn't get the chance. Friend Girl wasn't getting enough attention.

"You guys are upsetting my *stomach!*" she said, and shoved her plate away. A mostly-empty plate, I might add. "I can't even finish my *veggie* burger now!"

"Dude, that fucking does it," Boyfriend Guy said, and started scooting out of his side of the booth.

"These guys aren't *worth* it Mike, just *ignore* them." This from Phone Girl, as she steps aside to clear a path for him to lunge at Dave with no warning. It made me wonder if she did the same thing during sex. *I don't want to get pregnant Mike,* she whispers as she pulls his unused condom off.

"Screw that," Boyfriend Mike said. "I'm gonna kick some ass. That's what I do."

The guy was a fucking Neanderthal, and a badly clichéd Neanderthal at that. Who says that kind of stuff with a straight face? I looked at Lucas, our Neanderthal, to see if he was paying attention yet. "That guy is totally looking for trouble," I said.

Lucas looked at me. "You think?"

Boyfriend Mike stood up. "Damn straight I am," he said, tugging his jean shorts out of his crotch.

"Then it's your lucky day," Dave said. "Because Trouble is my confirmation name."

The roid-rage was beginning to creep in to the frat rat's neck. "Bring it on, bitch. Any time you're ready."

Dave stood up, pulled his pants up, and started going through his whole routine. He hopped up and down on the balls of his feet, did a bunch of elaborate stretches, shook his hands and arms out, jerked his head from side to side like a prizefighter. This cracked me up. I've known Dave since grade school, and he's never been in a fight in his life. Ever. He was probably stalling for time until Lucas would get up and save him, but Lucas was looking at the word puzzle on the placemat in front of him and cracking his knuckles the weird way, pressing on the tops of his fingers with the thumbs of the same hand, from index to pinky and back again, then popping the thumb with his fingers.

"Fuckin' make a move," Boyfriend Mike said, holding his fists close to his stomach. The classic indication of readiness, a sure sign that the fighter in question has seen too many karate movies and doesn't actually know shit from shampoo about organized fighting disciplines.

"No *you* make a move," Dave countered.

"Come on—"

"No *you* make a move. No *you* make a move. No *you* make a move. *You fucking make a move!*" Dave yelled. People were starting to look at us. "This part of the fight is always so awkward," he said to me, casting a sidelong glance in Lucas' direction.

"If you don't start something," Boyfriend Mike said, "I'm gonna finish it."

It probably made perfect sense in his mind, but it made us laugh. Dave picked up the guy's plate and grinned at him.

"Would you hit a man with glasses?" he said, pushing his up with his free hand.

"Fuck yeah."

Dave slammed the plate into Phone Girl's face and started rubbing it around, getting ketchup and lettuce and tomatoes and onions all over her. She, naturally, started screaming. Her friend did too. Friend Girl didn't want anybody to forget that she was girly and fragile and supposed to be hot, even though she had a weird face that looked like the third generation of inbreeding in the Swiss Family Robinson.

Boyfriend Mike was in shock. He'd been all braced for a block and counterattack, and then he's standing there, tensed up like a date-raping erection, and his girlfriend has got his leftovers all over her face and tits. It didn't take him long to recover, though. He drew his arm back and nailed Dave hard, right in the face.

Dave hit the floor like a sack of wet clay, but he was laughing, so I knew he wasn't hurt too bad. When I turned around to see what Lucas was going to do, he was already up and had Boyfriend Mike by the shirt.

Boyfriend Mike was fucked, and you could tell from the look on his face that he knew it. Lucas is big. Like, insane, monster big. 6'3", 285 lbs. I'm not going to lie and say that he's not fat, but under that fat is way too much muscle for one person who doesn't work out to have. He's a behemoth. He towered over Boyfriend Mike by a good four inches, and more than that after the third or fourth time he hammered him in the face and the guy's legs went slack. Lucas held him up by his frat shirt and just kept drilling him. Blood was flying all over the place.

Dave was trying to get up, but he was laughing so hard he couldn't get past his knees. Finally he grabbed Phone Girl around the waist and started rubbing his bloody nose all over her white shirt. She kept smacking him, but he wouldn't let go. The backs of her knees hit the booth and she fell, and he was still on top of her, smearing his blood all over those fantastic tits. That shirt was ruined, no question.

By this time, everybody in the restaurant was crowded on either end of the aisle, watching Lucas break Boyfriend Mike into Greek pieces. "Jesus Christ," some old farmer guy said. "He's gonna kill him."

He didn't sound too upset about it.

I scraped up my change and walked over the tables and the backs of the booths to get to the door. Dave grabbed Phone Girl's boobs--one in each hand--squeezed them like bicycle horns, complete with the "honk-honk," and came running behind me.

I don't know what Lucas did to him, but as I was pushing out the door to the parking lot I heard Boyfriend Mike scream like a woman—-

"My arm! Oh God, my fucking arm!"

I was still hungry.

2

<u>Pete</u>

I don't know how Lucas got to be the leader. We never held any kind of election among the three of us, and if Dave and Lucas had one, I never heard anything about it. No one ever came right out and said "Lucas, you're in charge," but he was, and all three of us knew it. If there *had* been an election, I'm pretty sure he wouldn't have put his name in the hat. Lucas is not a popularity kind of guy, or a persuader, or even a charmer. In fact, Lucas is an asshole. I would go on record with that. I've told him that a bunch of times, to his face, even though he could probably rip my head off my neck and then jam my face down onto the stump so the last thought that went through my brain was *Holy shit, I'm drowning in my own blood.* It doesn't seem to have any effect on him whatsoever. Telling him, I mean.

You can't hold a conversation of any length with Lucas unless you do all the talking, because on average he only lets off about ten sentences a day, and most of them are seven words or less. Whole weeks have gone by where I couldn't remember at the end of it if he'd said anything at all. You'd think that kind of silence would get annoying after awhile-- and it does--but whenever he says anything I usually find myself wanting to tell him to fuck off and shut up, so his silence is usually something to be thankful for.

Dave, on the other hand, never shuts up. If you don't stop him, he'll just keep talking and go off on these weird tangents about stuff that make me laugh until my stomach and face muscles hurt. Either he's a genius, or there is something seriously wrong with him and he needs to be heavily medicated and kept away from television.

Case in point:

We were walking down Pierce Street after the whole restaurant fiasco, arguing about whether or not all soratory chicks are named Jen. Somewhere Dave had gotten this particular idea into his head, and he wouldn't let go of it.

"You're full of shit," I told him.

"It's a proven theory."

"Are you listening to this crap?" I asked Lucas. He was casing houses and didn't bother to look at me.

"He helped do the research," Dave said.

I lit a cigarette--Newport Menthol, not those shitty Winston Light old-man cigarettes that Lucas smokes and Dave bums off of him. "So you're telling me that all soratory girls are named Jen. I can walk by any soratory house and yell 'Hey, Jen,' and they're all gonna turn around?"

"Not all of them," Lucas said, looking up at a second story window with a light in it. The blinds were slatted the wrong way and I could see some little girl's kitty poster on the wall. "Maybe half."

"I'd say more like 86%," Dave argued. "Give me a cigarette."

I gave him one. "So what you're asking me to believe is that you actually did a case study and came to the brilliant conclusion that, more times than not, American females named Jennifer, upon entering an institution of higher learning, will be inclined to join a sorority. And you have statistics on this. On paper."

"Fuck 'on paper,'" Dave said, complete with quote-fingers, as he handed my lighter back to me. "You don't have to put something on paper for it to be true."

"I never put down on paper that you're an asshole," Lucas said. I'm not sure which one of us he was referring to, but I assumed it was me.

"I write that in my diary all the time," Dave said. "But it's registered in the Library of Congress that I have a large penis, which proves beyond a shadow of a doubt that putting something down on paper doesn't necessarily make it so."

"What are you talking about?" I said, already starting to lose my temper. Dave's brand of logic will do that to you. I think because it doesn't actually contain any logic.

"There's all sorts of crap written down that's wrong. That home remedies book said to gargle with salt water to help a sore throat, but I swallowed some of it and puked and then had to eat again, which made my throat hurt worse. God*damn* it. The Bible, and algebra books? There's no way all that's true. *T.V. Guide*'s wrong sometimes, and it's printed on paper."

"Had I realized how much importance you were going to put on the word 'paper' in my argument--"

"You weren't arguing," Lucas said. After delivering a good beating, the guy was a regular blabbermouth. "You were being a bitch."

"And by that you mean you didn't publish your findings."

Dave kicked a flat Dr. Pepper can on the sidewalk and sent it skittering into the street. "What can I say? *Playboy* wanted pictures, too."

"Of you?"

"No, those came back unopened." He took another drag off my cigarette and shook his head. "Fucking fascists."

See what I mean? Arguing with him about anything is as productive as masturbating with a fork.

3

Pete

We heard the car coming, but I was the only one who went to the window to check it out. Dave was watching TV and Lucas was off doing whatever it is he did in some other part of the house. "Thumb that down," I said, and Dave muted the TV with the remote.

It was a wine-red Mustang, one of the newer ones. I like those. They look classy. They're also about $40,000, which puts them way out of any price range I'll ever be in. The Mustang pulled up to the curb and a frat rat opened the door just in time for the brunette in the back seat to stagger out, trip over a crack in the sidewalk, and puke all over the front lawn. It was a three-hurker, mostly liquid. Another night for the precious college memories scrapbook, no doubt.

I cracked the front window, one of those ones you open with the crank at the bottom, so I didn't miss anything good. When the girl in the passenger seat leaned over Mustang Guy I could see she looked almost like Puking Girl. *"Eeewww!"* she said. "Are you gonna be okay?"

Puking Girl was staggering around in a circle, probably trying to remember which way she'd put her Tampax in. "No..." she groaned, smacking her chops. "I just *bought* this dress... why is puke so *dirty?"*

"We're gonna go to that after-ups on Chandler," Mustang Guy's girl said. "So if you feel better, page me hon, 'kay?"

Puking Girl nodded, then doubled over and spilled her guts again before waving goodbye to her best friends for life, who were already hauling ass. There were eight concrete steps from the sidewalk up to the front walk and door of the house, and Puking Girl missed all of them at least once. I cranked the window shut, watched her dig around in her little slut purse for her keys for a minute, then flopped down on the couch with Dave.

"Where's Lucas?" I said.

Dave shrugged. "Why the hell is *I Love Lucy* on all the time? Does anybody really like that shit?"

"Somebody must, or they wouldn't still be playing it."

"Nobody likes homework, but people still do it," Dave said. "And herpes isn't much fun either, so I'm told, but people get it all the time."

"What's your point?"

"You're short," Dave said, and started flipping channels again.

I don't know how long it took Puking Girl to figure out that the door wasn't locked, or even latched, but she finally staggered against it and tripped over the doorjamb. "Hi," she said, flashing us a rippling, drunken smile that was all lips. Her eyelids looked like they weighed 5 lbs. each. "Who are you?"

"Jen's friends," Dave said.

"Oh, cool," Puking Girl said, and held down most of a thick, wet burp. "Which Jen?"

Dave let out one of his cackles, and Puking Girl's face muscles gave out for good. She still looked pretty hot, even though the corners of her mouth were trying to touch her knees.

"Puked, huh?" I said, trying to get some kind of conversation going. There is no bad time to practice your chick skills. "That's a bitch. I bet your stomach's had quite a workout today, what with you already forcing up the salads you had for lunch and dinner."

She looked at me, I think. The way her eyes were swimming, it was hard to tell. "I didn't puke after *lunch.*" She put her hand on the wall to steady herself, knocked a framed group shot of the sorority off-kilter, and focused on Dave. "What's up with your *head,* dude?"

Dave swiped his fingers across his forehead and held them up to the glow of the TV. There was blood on them, blue-black in the flickering light. I looked over the back of the couch to make sure the girls were still there and not moving, and they were. At least what was left of them.

"It's been one of those nights," Dave said. "One big mess after another."

"It looks like *blood,*" Puking Girl said. This struck her as funny and she began to laugh, which made her tits jiggle nicely inside her dress. Wash the puke off her, and I would totally have done her. "That's *gross,*" she said. "You have a gross head, dude."

"At least my head's still attached," Dave told her.

"What does *that* me--?"

Lucas came out of the shadows beside her and hacked into her throat with a meat cleaver we'd found hanging on one of those magnet strips in the kitchen. One swing nearly

19

took her head off. Puking Girl dropped hard, popping the back of her skull on the doorknob before she hit the floor and went into spasms. She didn't die right away; the blood just kept coming and the hole in her throat gurgled and sputtered for at least a minute, maybe more. Her feet and hands fluttered around like somebody had stuck a live wire up her ass.

Dave laughed. He jumped up off the couch and threw his arms up in the air. "That was classic! The German Judge gives it a 10!" he cried.

Lucas dropped the cleaver into the growing pool of blood on the carpet in front of Puking Girl's face and whipped his hand at the wall to get some of it off his glove. The red on white looked kind of cool until it all started to run together. Then it just looked like a mess.

I watched Dave kick the television off its stand and jump out of the way as the picture tube exploded. He started stomping the glass and kicking the cabinet, doing some weird little jig. "German judge?" I said. "I thought you were Irish."

"I am." He started doing something that looked like Riverdance and wasn't half bad, considering that he wasn't putting any effort into it. "I'm a covert agent for the IRA, posing as a German to sabotage the Olympic Games in an attempt to subvert national morale. It's a whole big thing, I'm not really supposed to talk about it. So like, this conversation never happened."

"I wish."

He grabbed me by the arms and put his face close to

mine. *"No,"* he said. *"*I'm serious. *This conversation never happened."*

4

Pete

There was a whole big thing on TV about us. They didn't know it was us, of course. Not that a lack of knowledge ever effected a TV newsman. One guy was on all the time, so he was the one I watched, because I freely admit that I'm self-absorbed and I have no problem with that. This guy, Todd Byrne, was a loser. He looked kind of like that big dopey guy who played the coach on *The White Shadow,* which Dave insisted on watching every day after we caught an episode where one of the basketball players got VD of some kind.

They had the soratory house fenced in with yellow tape, vehicles with flashing lights, and a bunch of blank-looking morons with open mouths waiting around hoping to catch a glimpse of skin when they wheeled the bodies out. Byrne was standing in front of the whole mess, trying to give the impression that he knew something about anything.

"As of yet authorities are playing it close to the vest, refusing to release any names until they can inform the few victims' families who have been unreachable up to this point. Friends and curious onlookers have been camped at the scene since news of this newest massacre broke early this morning, watching in horror as a seemingly endless stream of their classmates and sisters leave, never to return again.

"The events of last night are not clear, but what is clear is that the residents of this once peaceful college town could be looking over their shoulders for a long time to come." He paused so the viewing audience could let this sink in, which was nice of him. "This has been Todd Byrne, Action 8 News, live from the scene in Friedman, Illinois."

On and on like that, all afternoon. Sometimes they'd come on and say that some cop guy said this and that, and then they'd come back on fifteen minutes later and say that no one had said anything, that the previous information they'd given out had been incorrect. They interviewed a bunch of slack-jawed yokels and asked them stupid questions that had nothing to do with anything, then tried to work their dipshit answers into some kind of theory about what had happened and who had done it. There were a bunch of chicks crying and moaning and hugging each other. I recognized some of them from my lecture classes, but their makeup was all runny from bawling and none of them looked very hot.

I heard Lucas get up and grab a shower and shave. The house we lived in was a piece of shit, so between the fake wood paneling and 2x4 walls, the creaking floors and the antique ventilation system, you could hold your breath for two seconds and know what anybody in the house was doing. Lucas and I had bedrooms in the basement; he got the smaller one because he lost the coin toss. His head almost touched the ceiling, and with the furnished bed and dresser in there, there was a narrow path from the door to his tiny closet, which was full of books and had no door on it. My room was massive, way more space than anybody needed. I had two ceiling lights and a door on my closet, but a water pipe junction stuck out of the wall right over the head of my bed, so it wasn't all it was cracked up to be. Between braining myself when I was drunk, having to hear the gurgle of waste rushing past me every time somebody flushed the upstairs toilet, and the skittery-clicking of the roaches in the walls, I didn't get much in the way of restful sleep.

Lucas takes a long time to do his daily grooming. To look at the end result you'd think there wasn't much to it, but he's very methodical and thorough. He gets up, takes a piss, gets in the shower for about a half hour. Then he gets out, dries off, goes to his room, puts on a pair of underwear and his jeans, and goes back to the bathroom. He brushes his hair, which takes a good five minutes, because he's got a lot of it. Then he starts the water running for his daily shave, and while that's getting hot enough to boil noodles in, he cleans all the stray hairs out of the brush, blows his nose, stretches, and cleans his ears with Q-Tips. When the steam starts to overtake the mirror he plugs the drain and starts lathering up his face. He has sideburns and a goatee--no mustache--so all he shaves are the sides of his face, his neck, and his upper lip. He does this faster than you would think humanly possible; if it wasn't for having tough skin, he would probably have hacked pieces out of his face a hundred times over. Then he washes all the leftover shaving cream off, dries his hands, puts on powder deodorant (I've never been able to figure that one out,) washes his hands again and finishes dressing. Then he takes vitamins--a B-

Complex, three C's, an E, a multi-vitamin and a calcium--brushes his teeth, and then brushes his hair again. Then he puts a black t-shirt on, goes upstairs to the kitchen, gets three beers out of the fridge, lights a cigarette, puts his steel-toed boots on, and watches cartoons for at least an hour.

I listened to him go through this with the TV muted until I heard the floorboards in the living room creak when he sat down in his chair. Literally *his* chair. You could sit in it when he wasn't around, but if he came into the room and meant to sit down, you got up. Otherwise he would physically remove you from it and deposit you on the couch. Like your dad, if your dad happened to be a massive prick.

He was watching the news when I heard Dave get up and start going through his morning groans, muttering, and *"Ah, shits."* He tripped over something, probably one of the piles of magazines he keeps everywhere, and crashed into a wall, which lead to more groaning.

"Hey," he said when he finally made it into the living room.

"We made the news again." Lucas' voice is deep, and right after he wakes up you can barely understand anything he says.

"Really?"

"Every channel in the tri-state area."

I heard the floor thump as Dave flopped down on the couch. "Thank God *The Wonder Years* is on cable. Got another one of those?"

I knew Lucas was giving him a cigarette. It was the

routine of the day.

"So what do they say? Any leads?"

"No."

"Is that bitch Pete up yet?"

I turned off my TV and headed upstairs.

"I heard his stereo," Lucas said.

"Probably jerking off," Dave said. "Man, I slept like the dead."

"You and eight other people."

"Jesus Christ we're famous," I said, and flopped down on the couch next to Dave with a bottle of Sunny D. The California style. The Florida kind is shit.

"How'd you know?" Dave said. He blew a big drag in my face and grinned.

"I've been watching on my TV since one. We're fucking everywhere."

Dave pulled down the leg of his boxer shorts where it had ridden up on him and flicked ash into an empty Mountain Dew can. "How long till they give us some clever name like the Soratory Slicers or the Bitch...Butcher...ers?"

"They haven't even decided if it was more than one person," I said, lighting a smoke of my own. "Or if they have they're not saying. I think we prolly got away clean again. Because cops? Stupid."

Lucas stood up and dug in his pocket for his keys. "Where are you going?" I said.

"Beer run."

Dave finally got a piece of lint out of his bellybutton and threw it on the carpet. "What should we do if Geraldo calls?" he said.

"Take a message and tell him to practice looking outraged," Lucas said. "And ask if we can borrow money."

5

Pete

We went to a state university, but not one of the big ones. Not even one of the good ones. The school has this whole spiel they go through at every opportunity about how they may not be the most well-known university in the state, but that just helps the students by giving them access to a top-flight education at an affordable price. Hooray for us. It's so affordable, in fact, that no one seemed to notice that they raised tuition at least 3% every semester to pay for shit like a $10 million student rec center that nobody but jocks, frat rats and soratory sluts use. I do not lift weights, play racquetball, or enjoy the company of sweaty people who grunt a lot and high-five each other, but I still had to pay for their big fancy clubhouse. Hooray for Communism.

I was the only one of us who actually went to class on a regular basis. Lucas went on test days and Dave usually didn't even make those, but he was in the Art department, so he just did all his projects at home or slipped in through the storeroom window of the Heating Plant Annex, did them at night when no one was around, and turned them in pretty much whenever he felt like it. He usually passed the Art classes and failed everything else. I don't know what kind of grades Lucas made. He didn't talk about it.

Personally, I liked going to class. I'm not as well-read as I would like to be, and genuinely enjoy the educational process for the knowledge it provides. Dragging myself out of bed in the morning and hiking over to the campus was a pain in the ass, but once I got there everything usually worked out okay. There was an order in the act of taking notes on a lecture and studying them later that had a real calming effect on me. My brain went on autopilot and I didn't feel like anybody or anything. The whole world faded out except for the professor talking and whatever visual aids they might be using, and I could sit there for an hour or so like a smooth gray stone in the middle of a stream that washes all around me and moves on.

Some days I almost hated to go back to the house, but the Tuesday after Puking Girl, I was excited. The student newspaper was all over it, and I was freaking out. Everywhere I went people were talking about it. The whole campus was whispering and giving each other weird looks. Anybody remotely suspicious-looking got stared down and talked about.

The bizarre thing is, we live in America--home of Ted Bundy, Charles Manson and Ed Gein. As a country we've watched so many serial killer documentaries on cable that no one is above suspicion. The wild-looking guy with ragged clothes is always the first one you think of, but then all those TV shows kick in. You can't just look at a guy with nice clothes and an expensive haircut anymore and know that he didn't do it. It could be that handsome guy with the nice clothes and everything going for him. It could be the guy who rarely says anything but is always polite, almost meek. It could be the friendly businessman who always gives to charity, the slightly overweight moron stocking the vending machines who tries too hard to be your buddy when all you want is a package of Combos, the immigrant Sociology professor who somehow manages to keep his job year after year even though his English is a joke. Any of them could have done it. They could have all been in on it together, members of a secret little club that started sacrificing puppies to Satan one night a week for kicks and decided that just wasn't enough anymore.

Knowing who had done it--or more specifically, that *I* had done it--had my brain on overload. I sat in classes, listening to the talk around me, trying not to laugh out loud at how clueless they all were. You just wanted to jump up and scream, *"It was me, fuckheads! I did it! I killed them! And if my friend points at your house and nods his head some night, I'll do you too, and there's not a fucking thing any of you can do about it!"*

But of course you can't do that, so you just scream it to yourself over and over and hold your lips together to keep from laughing and drawing any unwanted attention to yourself. It's the funniest thing in the world, the joke that nobody's in on but you. But it's not without its drawbacks. A hot girl looks at you, and you don't know if she's into you or memorizing your description to give to the cops. A lull in conversation when you walk by, and you're positive they *know*, that *everybody* knows, and at any moment there will be a knock on the classroom door, a brief whispering conference with the professor, and you'll be hauled out in handcuffs for the viewing pleasure of a bunch of reporters and the home television audience. Your brain goes up and down like that all day long, and it nearly tears you apart. In a few days it fades and you almost feel normal again, until the next time.

People were more than happy to share their copies of the paper with you if you were sitting next to them, but nobody wanted to give it up. Usually you'd see perused copies lying around in the halls and under desks, but we were good for business. We made that piece of shit paper a collector's item among the student body every time we subtracted a few of their number, and finding a copy was impossible. I looked all over campus and finally found one on the floor of the student union, hidden under a pile of red Domino's Pizza inserts that everyone had let drop out of the center of the paper in their hurry to get to the death toll. Domino's was offering some good deals, but I doubt their business was too good. Nobody wanted to open their door to a stranger after dark anymore, stupid red and blue uniform or not.

When I got back to the house Lucas was sitting in his chair, drinking Killian's Red and watching *Thundercats*. His hair was still wet and he was blowing smoke through the slats of sunlight filtering in through the blinds, watching it roll.

I dropped my backpack on the floor with the rest of the crap and dug the paper out of it. "You go to class today?"

He shook his head and blew another puff. Lucas always looked too clean after a shower, unnatural. He wet-brushed his hair straight back, away from his face, so it was disorienting to see his whole face, like seeing Dave without his glasses on.

"It was fucking awesome," I told him. "They're canceling class Friday in honor of those chicks. Fucking three-day weekend! Do you believe that shit?"

"Somebody's daddy must have had some bucks," he said.

"Everybody's going crazy. There's a big story in the paper about them kicking, then the rest of it is a big tribute to the eight of them, pictures and life stories and everything. I had to look everywhere for one. People wrote a bunch of crappy poetry about missing them and drew hearts and shit all over the sidewalks in chalk, it was pathetic. And there are flyers all over the place about how they're gonna have another Take Back the Night rally."

One corner of Lucas' mouth went up. "That should keep them safe," he said. "Nothing more intimidating than folk songs and marching."

"Where's Dave?" I asked.

"In bed."

"I'm gonna wake him up. He'll wanna see this."

I shook Dave awake and waited for him to find his glasses and put them on before shoving the paper in his face. He frowned at it and tried to get his eyes to clear for a couple seconds, tracing the lines of print with his finger. When he got to the end of the first paragraph he threw the paper back at me and pounded both fists on the mattress, then stood up and started bouncing.

"Fucking awesome!"

6

Pete

What scares people most about murder is that they can't figure it out. There's no reality to it. There's a reality in a dead body, because you can prove that it's no longer living. You can measure and weigh it, check the brainwaves or the body temperature or the heartbeats per minute, and write all the figures down. Once facts and figures are determined, reality is born.

A dead body is concrete; murder is abstract. It's all in the mind. Murder is a particle and murder is a wave. Statistics do not apply. There aren't any numerical calculations that can be done where at the end of them you can come up with a final answer that will tell you who has the highest probability of taking another human life. It just doesn't work that way.

I'm not sure how it works for us. There are no discussions, no questions, no invitations. With a loaded gun pressed behind my ear the best reason I could come up with is that we go where Lucas goes and follow his lead. The same excuse the Nazis offered at the end of World War II. Nobody bought it then, either.

After I showed Dave the paper he took a shower and put on clean clothes because, "As a figure just out of sight of the public eye, I owe it to myself to maintain a certain level of mainstream presentability. Is that even a word? Anyway, my head's starting to itch and my armpits smell like dead woodchucks."

What Dave's hygiene lacks in quantity he tries to make up for in quality, so I read the paper from front to back--even the sports page--and watched cartoons with Lucas for an hour or so until Dave was done cleaning himself. Then when he got dressed he cooked himself four hamburgers and challenged us to a *Mortal Kombat II* tournament, so we all went to my room and played that for a couple of hours. We're all pretty good at it, but it's my game, so I spend a lot of time practicing when I can't sleep because it feels like cheating, and cheating is always pleasurable. Usually I can pull some special move out of my ass if I'm on the third match and things aren't looking good, although I have be careful. You can rip Lucas' guy's head off or something and he doesn't mind, but if you turn him into a baby or make paper dolls out of him, he'll punch you in the chest. And that fucking hurts.

After *Mortal Kombat II* we watched *21 Jump Street.* Dave cooked two more hamburgers for himself and one for me. Lucas had six more beers and polished off a pack of cigarettes. Then Lucas started reading *Transformer,* the biography of Lou Reed, Dave tried to figure out how to play "Father to a Sister of Thought" on his guitar, and I did my Oceanography homework.

At 9:30 Lucas stood up, stretched, and looked at us. Dave and I dropped what we were doing and followed him out the back door, down the alley that separates our side of the street from the fraternity row annex on the other side of the block, and toward the general direction of campus. Not many people were out, just the usual freaks and band kids coming home from practicing late to keep their scholarships. Everybody was looking everybody else over without trying to be obvious about it. There was no way of knowing when your description of somebody might make you a TV hero, and nobody wanted to throw away their ticket for that particular once-in-a-lifetime lottery.

A bunch of black kids were hanging out in front of the student union with one leg of their sweatpants pulled up to the tops of their calves and the other all the way down, sweating inside their big parkas and talking extra ghetto to prove to themselves that they hadn't sold out by paying money to be educated with Whitey.

They were obnoxious, but when Lucas walked past they all went quiet and stared him down hard. That's when I noticed they were wearing military boots, spray painted gold. In one of the black frats there was supposed to be a secret club--the Q-Dogs--that you had to earn your way into by beating down a white guy or raping a white girl. Q-Dog pledges wore gold boots. I'd heard all of this and shrugged it off as some kind of racist rumor, because it sounded too retarded to be true. Apparently it was not only true; it was about to happen to us.

It still seemed retarded.

I looked around, saw nobody, and started to get jittery. I'm a decent fighter with somebody about my size, one-on-one, but these guys were all bigger than me and outnumbered us two to one. If anything happened, I was going to get my ass kicked.

"What the fuck you lookin' at?" one of them said. A white lollipop stick poked out of the corner of his mouth.

Lucas stopped. "You talking to me?"

"Yeah motherfucker, I'm talking to you."

"Don't," Lucas told him, and started to move on.

The Q-Dogs moved around a little bit but didn't seem to go anywhere. Lollipop Stick took a step forward, at an angle toward the back of Lucas' shoulder. "Don't what?"

Lucas turned on him like he had all the time in the world, and I knew from the look on his face this wasn't going to be one of those things we would just walk away from and bitch about later. He took the thumb and middle finger of his right hand, put them to his forehead and pared his bangs back from his face. Lucas has got the hardest eyes I've ever seen. Superman can burn holes in steel, but Lucas can look at you and make you feel like you're going to shit your pants.

"Don't talk to me," he said. "Don't look at me. Don't think about me. And unless you're counting on some of your fudge-packing butt brothers to come down here and pick your sorry Tupac-loving asses up off the goddamn sidewalk and carry you home, don't take another step in my fucking direction. That clear enough for you, sweetie?"

Silence. The Q-Dogs stared at him like he was from another planet, maybe one where white boys are born insane and grow worse with age. I felt like I was going to vomit.

Somebody had to say something, and since Lollipop Stick had put himself out front, it was his turn. "Where I come from, fat white boys with pretty little girl hair don't be comin' out after dark and trying to talk shit. We scalp them motherfuckers like motherfuckin' Indians."

General agreement and cheering from the Q-Dogs, with a couple of barks thrown in for good measure. This was a witty bunch, no doubt about it.

"Then you're a long way from home," Lucas told him, and Dave laughed. It was not infectious.

I didn't know Lucas had a knife. And I have absolutely no idea how he got it out and open that fast. It wasn't a switchblade or a stiletto--it was a good old fashioned redneck buck knife, with a blade five inches long and an inch wide. He snapped his wrist and the blade locked open with a click, the point touching the tender skin below Lollipop Stick's left eye.

Everybody flipped out, but nobody moved. I think we were all afraid to. I know Lollipop Stick was. His mouth started to yammer, but instead of words all that came out was his stick, with a shriveled red pebble on the end of it. He seemed to be blinking 40 times per second. Lucas stood perfectly still and waited.

"Cool out!" Lollipop Stick finally stammered. "Just cool the fuck out, man. Don't fuck around and be makin' me lose my motherfuckin' eye over some shit. We's just playin'. Ain't we just playin'?"

The other future Q-Dogs agreed wholeheartedly.

"What game is this." It didn't sound like a question, the way Lucas said it. He pressed the tip of the knife into skin and gave it a gentle turn. In the glow of the streetlight I could see a teardrop of thick red blood slide down Lollipop Stick's cheek.

"I don't know man," Lollipop Stick moaned. "Don't cut my eye, man. I'm beggin' you, don't fuckin' cut my shit."

Lucas leaned forward so that his face was only six inches from Lollipop Stick's. "Billy Goat's Gruff," he said. With his empty hand he brought his hand up and tugged at his goatee. "You're the Q-Goats, and you want to cross my bridge."

"Q-Goats!" Dave snorted. "Fucking awesome."

Lollipop Stick's eyes darted toward Dave and I; Lucas pressed in with the knife again. "If you want to look at anything tomorrow, you better look at me now. You're the Q-Goats and you want to cross my bridge. Let me hear it."

"We wanna cross yo' bridge," Lollipop Stick said, his voice barely above a whisper.

"No."

"What?"

"That's not what I said. Use good diction, for fuck's sake. And repeat it like I said it. All of you."

The Q-Dogs glanced at each other and shifted uneasily. Two of them were big, almost Lucas' size, but none of them seemed to be in a hurry to rush him.

"One more push, and your eyeball's going in a Cool Whip container in my fridge," Lucas said. "Forget about the pain. Forget about having to wear a glass eye and have everybody stare at it for the rest of your life. Think about how you're going to explain to your mom and dad that after they worked and saved to send your sorry ass to college so that you could work hard and make something of yourself, you lost your eye because you were out acting like a fucking *gangsta* to impress a bunch of no-good arrogant cocksuckers who won't give you the time of day unless you pay them to. Think about that. Because I am not fucking with you. I'll pop your eye out and eat it right here and now, just to make sure nobody can put it back. You wanted to play, we're playing. Now hold your fucking end up."

I looked at Dave to see what his reaction was to this Lucas version of the Gettysburg Address. He was already staring at me, his eyebrows peeking over the tops of his glasses and a shocked grin on his face. Parts of this speech would be repeated around our house for months.

"We are the Q-Goats," Lollipop Stick said, carefully enunciating each word with his stained red lips and tongue. "We want to cross your bridge."

"Wait, wait," Dave said. "We have to do this right. Can I be the troll? I mean, I know nature already decided that Pete was, but can I pretend?"

"Fuck you," I said. I wanted this over. OPS--the Office of Public Safety, i.e. the campus cops--had their office a block away, and the last thing any of us needed was to get caught with Lucas sticking a knife in a kid's eye. And the fact that nobody had come out of the student union yet was beyond insane. Usually the place had people coming and going from open to close.

Lucas nodded. He kept his eyes on Lollipop Stick's.

"Who's that trippy-trapping on my bridge?" Dave bellowed, leapt forward, hands splayed like he meant to choke someone. The Q-Dogs all jumped. They looked like they were dangerously close to involuntary bowel movements.

"We are the Q-Goats," they said in near-unison. "We want to cross your bridge."

"Nope, sorry," Dave said, and I wanted to kick the crap out of him.

"Pay the toll," Lucas said.

"How much?" one of the Q-Goats asked.

"One pair of gold boots each. Take 'em off."

"And tie the laces," Dave ordered. He was really getting a kick out of it. "I don't want to drop them on the way back to my troll house."

There was a pause. "How we gonna walk home with no shoes?" Lollipop Stick asked. "Come on, man."

Dave laughed. "Confucius say: Better to walk home with no shoes than with one eye. At least I think he said that. It might have been Conan O'Brien."

"Now." Lucas didn't raise his voice, but he didn't have to. His intent was loud enough.

The Q-Dogs, with the exception of Lollipop Stick, rushed to untie their boots and kick them off. "I can't do it with that knife in my eye, man," Lollipop Stick said. "Don't cut me, man. I can't reach them."

Lucas waved a hand in our direction and Dave and I started picking up boots. "You get to keep yours," he said.

"Say what?"

Lucas swiped a finger down Lollipop Stick's cheek and held it up. The blood looked like paint. "You already paid.

These gutless motherfuckers left you hanging out to dry. You remember that. Say it."

The muscles around Lollipop Stick's eyes flexed. "These gutless motherfuckers left me hanging out to dry," he said. He wasn't just repeating it; he meant it.

"This is done."

"This is done," Lollipop Stick said. "Yes sir, it's done and then some."

Lucas pressed the lock latch at the base of the knife handle and folded the blade back in. "Take off."

The Q-Dogs went in a hurry, hobbling down the sidewalk in their socks. Lollipop Stick was last. "Thanks for not takin' my eye," he said. His voice was shaky; the words were precise and abrupt, as if he needed to get them out and over with but wanted to be sure he got them right. "I ain't doin' no shit like this again, swear to God."

Lucas nodded and the knife went back into his pocket. He turned back toward home without looking at us and we followed him; Dave had three pairs of boots and I had two. "Yeah," I said. "And what are we supposed to do with five pairs of spray-painted boots?"

"You could plant flowers in them and set them out along the front sidewalk," Dave said. "Although somebody's bound to see them and go tell the Q-Goats, which means they'll come over some night and kick your ass."

"What? Why would they just kick my ass? Why not yours?"

"Because you're the smallest, and you suck the most, and I'll pay Lucas a dollar to protect me."

"I'll pay him ten dollars," I said. "And I know you don't have ten dollars, so that means you're gonna take a beating."

"No, you don't understand," Dave said. "I offered him *a dollar*. One dollar American."

"Yeah, and I'm saying *ten dollars,* American, which is more than one dollar in any country."

"Lucas, we need a ruling here."

Lucas didn't turn around. "The bidding is closed."

"Hah," I said. "That means I win."

Dave grinned. "Not so fast, slapnuts. Don't you ever go on eBay? This auction has been ended with the Buy It Now feature. Once an offer has been made, the sale is final and no more bids can be accepted."

"You are so full of shit."

"It's true. You're just jealous because I got a lot of entertainment value for my dollar."

"What entertainment value?"

"I get to watch you get your ass kicked by a bunch of black guys, and the guarantee that nothing will happen to me. It'll be better than TV, almost. At least there won't be any commercials just when it's getting to the good part. I won't have to watch anything about Tampax between the time they pull their knives out and the time they start stabbing you. Unless your tampon falls out, I guess, in which case you have more problems than I care to discuss at this hour of the night."

"Why is it that every time I talk to you I end up wanting to physically hurt you?" I asked.

"Beats me," Dave shrugged. "Not that you could or anything. But don't feel bad, it's not your fault. It's hard to be intimidated by a midget who wears a cuntrag."

"I fucking hate you," I said calmly, "and I'm not a midget."

"Did they raise the height requirement for being a midget?"

"I'm going to kick your ass."

"No you won't."

"Why not?"

"Because you can't catch me," Dave said. "I'll just run to the amusement park and get on the roller coaster, and the big fat ugly guy who runs it won't let you in because the top of your head is below the line."

"He'll let me in," I said. "He knows me. He bangs my mom."

"Then I'll tell him you're pregnant," Dave said.

"But it's obvious that I'm male, and therefore can't be pregnant," I told him. "Your whole theory is full of holes, and you're an ass."

"Possibly," he nodded. "But it beats the theory that my asshole is full, and I can live with that."

Jesus Fucking Christ.

7

Pete

Thursday, the day of the Take Back the Night rally, was when everything went to shit. Lucas had a 9am class, 20th

Century British Literature or something like that, and he had an essay test that day, so he had to go. I think he ended up getting an A on it, but I have no idea how. He'd taken half a ten-strip of blotter acid at 11:00 in the morning on Wednesday and the rest of it while he watched *Thundercats,* which comes on at 3:30. He had to have been tripping his balls off, and I know he didn't sleep. I got up on Thursday morning for my Modern Social Problems class in time to watch him drain half a bottle of frozen gin on his way out the door. This in itself was amazing--he'd polished off a bottle of Aristocrat before I'd gone to bed, and the bottle he threw in the general direction of the trashcan as he stuck his ink pen in his back pocket and headed to class had been a full, sealed bottle of Beefeater.

Now I'd taken acid a few times, and I knew that it cuts the effects of alcohol down to almost nothing, if the acid is good. If you're knocking them back and drop just one hit, you don't feel bad at all. But ten hits and two bottles of gin... man. That threw me for a loop, and I've seen Lucas take anything and everything. The way he smelled when he walked past me, I thought he'd be lucky to make the block and a half trip between our house and the English building without collapsing from heart failure. We didn't have any air conditioning in the house, so he'd been sweating gin for seventeen hours straight. If I'm drinking hard liquor I know it's time to quit when I bring the bottle up to my face, get a whiff, and my stomach locks up. I was sober as a judge that morning, and my gut knotted so tight when he walked past me that it didn't completely relax until almost lunchtime.

Since I've known him, Lucas has never blacked out, passed out, thrown up, or even had a hangover. His constitution is the worst miracle modern science will never be able to discredit. Usually he exists on vitamins and peanut butter, which he eats plain, without bread--he just takes a spoonful and swallows it. Everything else he consumes is either drug-related, alcohol-related, or Mountain Dew, all of it accompanied by a steady diet of Winston Lights. And no matter what's running through his system he's always perfectly functional and coherent, at least on the outside. He doesn't scratch imaginary spiders off of his arms or start talking and trail off in mid-sentence; he doesn't even slow down or walk funny on codeine or horse tranquilizers. Whatever the drugs do to him, or for him, he keeps to himself. Dave, who drinks but refuses to use any kind of illegal drugs, likes to ask him at random what he's taken since the last time he woke up. The laundry list of chemicals, pills and smoke Lucas rattles off is frightening and disgusting in its quantity. By all measures of common sense and medical science, Lucas should have been pronounced dead 100 times over.

I peeked out the front door curtains and watched him until he was out of sight; for a minute I thought about following him just in case this was going to be the day he finally pushed himself over the limit and needed somebody to help him out. I ate a bowl of cereal instead. Lucas was my friend, for whatever reason, but if he was going to flip out, I didn't want to be anywhere nearby when it happened. If he got it, he'd been asking for it for a long time, and it was no business of mine.

That was all well and good in theory. By the time I got my shit together and was ready to leave for class, my head was spinning thinking about any number of things that could or might be happening to Lucas in that state. The kind of acid Lucas dropped wasn't the standard frat-boy-Grateful-Dead-fan-Friday-night shit. He'd given me two hits of it once and I peaked for 15 hours; the trip was so bad I'd actually considered suicide for the first and only time, just to get off of it. Finally Lucas took pity on me and fed me a handful of D-12 vitamins and some kind of home remedy cocktail that was Ny-Quil based so I could pass out until it was over. I could still remember the whole thing, crystal clear, and it still scared the hell out of me.

I wanted to wake Dave up and see if I couldn't get him to go over to the English building and make sure everything was okay, or hang around outside and wait for Lucas to come out and then walk him home or something. But waking Dave up suddenly is an all-day job, and I had to go.

I should have just stayed at the house. I couldn't pay attention for shit. On Tuesdays and Thursdays I had three classes, so I went to Soc and Biology, which both had strict attendance policies, and skipped Art History, which didn't.

When I got back to the house Lucas and Dave were in the living room watching *The A-Team*. At least that was what was on the TV. Dave was watching Lucas tear the pages out of his copy of *Mrs. Dalloway*, torch them with his lighter, and drop them into a half-eaten bowl of Sugar Smacks that had been sitting around so long there was skin on the top of it.

"That's impressive," I said. "Don't you know it's wrong to destroy literature?"

Lucas threw a page at me--one he hadn't started burning yet, thankfully--and said "Oh yeah. It's such fun to read. Virginia Woolf really pumps my nards."

"Holy shit!" Dave hooted. "A *Breakfast Club* reference! I haven't heard one of those in years."

"Why are you doing that?" I said. "They're not gonna buy it back if you trash it up like that."

"Not gonna anyway," Lucas said. He closed the book, grabbed it by the paperback spine, and ripped it in half. "The dickhead said he wasn't teaching it next semester."

"I take it you didn't like it enough to want to keep it for your personal library," I said.

Lucas' pupils were so blown his eyes looked black. There was a thin rim of brown iris at the edge, and the rest looked like somebody had drilled holes in his eyes and covered them with glass. If I'd gotten close enough to him, I might have been able to look in and see the flaming ball of hell that was his brain. He stared at me, the ends of his hair fluttering back and forth over his shirt pockets in the breeze coming through the raised window. Walking back and forth to class had blown some of the gin smell off of him, but not enough.

"You should take a shower," I told him, very careful to keep my tone from anything that resembled threats or mockery. "No offense, but you reek."

"Yeah," Dave nodded. "I never thought I would encourage anybody else to shower, but you're kind of ripe."

Lucas stared at a spot in the cheap wood paneling over

the back of the couch. "I wanna rip that shit down and trash it," he said. "Just chop the fuck out of it and stomp it till it's nothing but splinters."

Dave looked at me and cocked a hopeful eyebrow; I shook my head. "Nah, we better not," he said. "There's probably insulation behind it, and that stuff itches."

"Why would you want to do that anyway?" I said. "This place is a shithole, but that's not going to help it any."

"It's cheap and ugly," Lucas said. "It's cheap and ugly now, and it was cheap and ugly when they put it up."

"True," Dave said. "But ripping it to pieces is not going to raise the monetary value of it. And aside from the momentary beauty of pure destruction for its own sake, it's not gonna make it any prettier."

Lucas didn't so much stand up as rocket from his ass to his feet, the two halves of *Mrs. Dalloway* dropping from his fists. His pupils were blown open so wide it made my own eyes hurt to look at them. "If we tear it down," he said, "they'll have to put up something else. They can't leave it like that. If the Tenant Union shows up on one of those surprise inspections, they'll get fined out the ass."

Our landlords were a redneck yuppie couple who had only been to the house once since we'd moved in, to complain about the crop circles Dave had left in the yard when it was his turn to mow. When they asked--with that good old-fashioned condescending landlord false cheer--if our lawnmower was broken, Lucas told them that he'd needed the blade to take care of some stray dogs that had been digging in our trash. Apparently he scared the hell out of them, because they left in a hurry and hadn't been back since. We left our monthly envelope of cash in their mailbox on time, they left us alone, and things went smoothly all the way around.

"But they're not gonna know it needs replaced unless somebody calls them and has them come over here," I said. I was a little nervous. The speed of movement that Lucas can produce in the blink of an eye is always unsettling to me. Large people aren't supposed to move that fast. It goes against the laws of nature. "And then they're not going to pay for it out of their own pocket, they'll make us pay for it. Why should we foot the bill for improvements on their house?"

"Yeah, fuck them," Dave said. He was starting to seriously take my side, finally. "Stick it to the man, Petey. Right?"

"Take no prisoners, take no shit," Lucas said. The strange lilt he put on it sounded vaguely familiar and made me wonder if he was singing. "Shower."

"Holy Lola," Dave said when he was gone. "Do you think he's ever going to take so much shit he just freaks out and doesn't make any sense at all?"

"That made sense to you?" I said. "Wanting to rip the paneling off the wall for no reason other than it's cheap and ugly?"

"Being decisive always makes good sense, especially when it comes to matters of home decorating," Dave told me. "Do you realize how many people spend good money getting someone else to make those decisions for them?"

"So you're saying Lucas could have a great future in home decorating?"

"Possibly. Especially if that family from *The Texas Chainsaw Massacre* moves again."

8

Pete

I don't know how anybody can sleep on ten hits of acid, but after a 45-minute shower, Lucas did. At least I think he did. He programmed his CD player to repeat The Psychedelic Furs' *All Of This And Nothing* album over and over again, cranked it up, locked his bedroom door, and we didn't see him again until 7:30 that night. I like The Furs, but six hours of anything is enough to drive me insane, and I was seriously weighing the possibility of kicking his door in and turning it off when it stopped and Lucas came out of his room, freshly dressed and looking like he was ready to do some serious damage.

I followed him upstairs and watched him take his vitamins with a bottle of Corona, trying to get a look at his pupils. They looked fairly normal, but we hadn't turned on any of the lights in the house yet and it was starting to get dim. When Dave came in to raid the fridge Lucas was leaning on the counter, staring out the window over the sink with a calm focus that gave me a bad, bad feeling. If you follow the old proverb, the only thing that could follow tranquility like that was a raging, life-taking storm of epic proportions. And in our case, you were kidding yourself if you didn't take the prospect of that literally.

Dave knew it too. "Oh God, this is gonna be fantastic," he said. "I love this look."

Lucas' eyes turned in his direction.

"I swear to crap," Dave said. "You are one sexy motherfucker. Right now? The way the last grayish light of the setting sun is frolicking across your brutal-yet-oddly-charming wasteland of a face? If one of us was a photographer, we could make a million dollars with one shot." He held up a pretend camera and began making clicking noises, darting back and forth in front of Lucas like a fashion photographer. "Yeah, that's it baby. Work it for me. Give me sexy, that's it. Give me brooding. Mysterious. Ah fuck it, just give me head."

Lucas looked at him and said nothing.

"Alright," Dave said. He forgot about his air-camera. "Somebody's gotta step up to the plate here. Come on you guys, I've got a boner. Who's turn is it?"

"You're fucking disgusting," I told him.

"And I'm a liar," Dave said. "I don't really have a boner."

"You don't know how thrilled I am to hear that," I said. "Really."

"But we might as well get something lined up now, while we're all here thinking about it," Dave said. "I plan to have at least one erection before I go to sleep tonight or tomorrow or whenever, and it's not going to suck itself."

There was some truth in that somewhere. "I don't see what that has to do with us," I said.

"We're friends," he said. "Friends should help each other,

Pete."

"This whole conversation is way too gay," I said.

"Well, when I'm talking to a homo, I like to make him feel comfortable." Dave opened the fridge and took out a package of garlic bologna. "We have to go to the store sometime soon. By the way, I ate your chips."

"Which ones?"

"All of them."

"What the fuck? I had three different bags. Two of them weren't even opened yet!"

"That'll teach you. Nobody needs to buy three bags of chips at one time. Not only is it greedy, it's bad nutrition." He cut slits in the edges of the bologna slices and put them in the microwave. "Oh yeah, I ate some of your Rice Krispy Square too."

"How much?"

"All that was left, whatever that was."

"That was a 5 lb. brick!"

"Yeah, so like, four and a half pounds, maybe?"

"Is there anything of mine you didn't eat?"

"Your soul," Dave shrugged. "Satan called dibs, and fair is fair."

I could smell that damn garlic bologna frying even through the microwave door. "Jesus Christ," I said. "Why don't you eat some real food, that doesn't reek like ass?"

"Because you're too cheap to buy any."

"Since when it is my responsibility to feed you?"

"Since my parents disowned me for hanging out with you."

"Your parents haven't disowned you, they just think you're a lazy asshole."

"They will, eventually," Dave said. He opened the microwave and took out the plate. The three slices of bologna had shriveled and crisped up into flesh cups. "It's only a matter of time. Does anybody have any bread, or am I gonna have to look at this shit while I eat it?"

Lucas tossed him my loaf of bread. "Thanks, Lucas," Dave grinned. "It's good to know I have at least *one* generous friend."

"He can afford to be generous," I said. "It's my fucking bread."

"It's not the cost of the gift that matters, it's the thought behind it. Jesus, were your parents savages or what? Have some fucking manners, asshole."

"Why don't you bite me?"

"No thanks," Dave said, raising the plate for display. "I've got it covered. Maybe later." He tore into the first sandwich with a crunchy ripping sound that turned my stomach. "So Lucas, how was your day? See anything of note?"

"A whole box of paper dessert plates."

His voice made me jump. Chain-smoking four packs of cigarettes and chugging two bottles of gin in a 24-hour period had not done wonders in the way of giving him a crystal clear tone and pitch. He sounded like a bad guy in the best Satan-inspired tradition, which I would laugh at in a movie, but coming out of his mouth it was just creepy, I think because he wasn't doing it on purpose and I knew that he was for real. I guess he grew up in some white trash backwater, and the inflections he put on words sounded wrong to my Chicago-suburb ears. He never said "insurance," for example--it was always "*in*-surance." "Antenna" was "*ann*-tenna," "Joliet" was "Jolly-*yet*," etc. When I first met him it took me two months to understand him to a degree that didn't require my asking him to repeat everything he said at least once.

"Okay," Dave said, "since Pete obviously either doesn't understand the rudimentary basics of casual conversation or doesn't care that I'm trying to eat over here, I'll ask. Why did you see a whole box of paper dessert plates?"

Lucas lit a cigarette and took a few slow drags on it, until I thought he wasn't going to answer. Finally he said, "Wax guards for tonight's candlelight march through town."

"Well, that's something," Dave said. "Have a march to show serial killers that you're not scared of them, but God forbid you risk getting an ouchie on your manicured hands. Jesus Christ. I thought I had absolutely no respect for those chicks on the internet who stuck lit candles in their asses, but in light of this, they might have a few redeeming qualities after all."

"I wouldn't be hasty about a judgment like that," I said. "That's still a pretty long way from redeeming, no matter what context it's in."

"At least those sluts are economical," Dave said. "They figured out how to get off and remove unsightly ass hair at the same time. These sluts just want to be a marching case of jock-itch. I mean, seriously, *Take Back the Night?* What the fuck? Take it back from who?"

"Us, I think."

"I didn't even know we had it," Dave said. He started on the last of his shit-sandwiches and dropped the plate on top of the junkyard in our sink. "If we do have it, where are we keeping it? The night is *big*. Like *really* big. Bigger than our house and the trunk of Lucas' car put together. There's no way we have the night. No way. And if we did, I would make sure it was dark all the time, because sunlight is hot, and it sucks."

"It's figurative," I replied, knowing that he knew that already.

"It's horseshit," Dave grunted around a mouthful of bread and mutilated garlic bologna. "Plus, if we've got it, it's ours. We took it fair and square. I say we rent some apes with Nazis on their backs, give them machine guns, and order them to disperse that parade with a maximum of unnecessary force."

"Let's not."

"Well can we at least throw some stink bombs at them?"

"No."

Dave sighed. "Okay, final offer. What if we get in Lucas' car, drive around, shout naughty words at them, and then peel out? That'll fix them."

I laughed, which was all he really wanted anyway. I think. With Dave, it's hard to tell.

"You done?" Lucas said.

We didn't know if he was talking about the asinine conversation or Dave's sandwiches from hell, but the answer was the same either way. "Yeah," we said.

Lucas walked out the back door.

"If my dad had the kind of understated heroic charisma Lucas has, what do you think I would have turned out like?" Dave asked.

"You'd probably be exactly the same," I said. "Only with a conscience, an ulcer, and a better grade-point average."

"So what you're basically saying is that I'm better off," Dave nodded. "That's what I thought too, but it never hurts to have a second opinion."

Lucas had already crossed the backyard and was in the alley. We raced each other out the back door; I thought I had it won when I body checked Dave into the doorjamb, but he recovered and kicked my legs out from under me when I tried to hurdle over a crop circle that had grown to an impressive 10 inches. Four rabbits having some sort of informal gathering froze underneath Lucas' Camaro, then took off toward the dumpsters behind the frat house across the alley and disappeared.

9

Pete

We headed over to the South Quad and watched all the chicks and their pussywhipped boyfriends stand around and cheer in all the appropriate places for a while. They had a couple of girl folk singers who might not have been bad if their subject matter was different. One of them was pretty hot, cats-eye glasses and blonde dreads with green streaks in them. And she was wearing a belly-shirt, which is always sexy when a girl doesn't actually have a belly.

A tubby lesbian chick with a bunch of piercings in her face was passing out pink glo-sticks so people could show solidarity with the BGLFA--the Bi-sexual, Gay, Lesbian and Friends Alliance--which Dave took two of and promptly stuck down the front of his pants just to piss her off. "I can't help it," he said apologetically. "Anytime I see something pink, I just want to touch it with my wiener."

That cracked me up, because let's face it, the word "wiener" is funny no matter how old you are. "Fucking sexist pigs," the tubby lesbian girl with all the shit in her face said, and stalked off to bother somebody else with her politically correct man-hating shenanigans.

"It's always sobering to be called a pig by a girl who looks like she ate the whole trough and forgot to wipe the shavings off her face," Dave said loudly. "I may reevaluate my whole value system. Thanks, baby. Can I get your number? I was thinking of turning my face into a tackle-box too, and I might need some advice."

"Turn it down," Lucas told him, and Dave shut up. He left the glo-sticks in his pants.

They had the chicks singing their feminist anthems, a few daughters of hippie mothers made speeches, the Dean of Women Students or some bullshit thing like that warned everybody that this was a night to let loose and get their hostilities out, but that they needed to respect themselves, the campus and the community and not do anything that would give the rally a bad name. Apparently there was a fear that anything remotely phallic would be torched and guys on the street would be mobbed and titty-slapped into submission, which doesn't sound all that bad if the chicks are hot, but these chicks weren't. We stood on the patio behind the student union for a while, smoking cigarettes and watching Cuntstock until we couldn't take anymore fun and had to jet.

If there is a system to the way Lucas picks a house, I never figured it out. Sometimes I would see one I thought was just begging for it, and when I told him he'd shake his head and keep moving. I saw three or four likely prospects as soon as we got off campus, but he didn't go for any of them. Dave finally got close to me and murmured that I should probably shut up.

"I don't know what's going on," he said so softly, for him, that it made me uncomfortable. "But I think when it happens it's gonna be insane."

We roamed up and down the side streets in no particular hurry, and nobody said anything. Even Dave was quiet, which is a miracle in itself. We'd cut down one street for a block, move over two blocks, go back three, take an alley. There was no pattern to it.

When the last of the sun dropped we could hear a big roar come from the direction of the campus. Lucas pointed to the right and we cut across in the middle of the block, slipping between houses until we were on Carroll Street. Lucas slowed up and leaned against a tree, lighting another cigarette.

"This is kind of high-traffic, isn't it?" I asked.

56

He nodded.

"So what are we doing."

"Wait for it."

We waited. Ten minutes later I heard it--low at first, but getting louder as they came. The candlelight march was on, and they were coming our way. They were shouting slogans and whooping, holding their free hands in front of them to keep the breeze from snuffing the candle flames. When they got close enough to make out what they were, I had to admit it was an impressive sight. The cops were out in full force, halting traffic on the side streets until they passed. The chicks owned the streets, for an hour or so anyway.

"Oh man," Dave groaned. "I'm on overload here. You have no idea how much I have to say about this."

"It'll keep," Lucas told him.

"Tell me there's some kind of brilliant master plan at work here, at least. Because if you brought me out here just to stand around and watch this fucking tampon parade and slap bugs off my neck, I'm gonna have to kick your ass."

"I might have to help him," I said.

Lucas took his last drag and flipped the butt into a patch of dying crabgrass nobody had bothered to mow in a long time. "I had a few ideas," he said.

"Yes!" Dave said. "Fan-fucking-tastic. Can I guess some of them?"

Lucas nodded.

"We follow the parade route, and hit as many houses as we can along the way, like a trail-of-blood type deal. Was that one of them?"

"Yeah."

"We track down all the organizers and big mouths of this whole thing. Was that one of them?"

"Yeah."

"Either one of those sound good," Dave said. "Which one are we gonna do?"

"Neither."

"Why the hell not?"

"Too much time and not enough hands."

"So what are we gonna do?"

One corner of Lucas' mouth twitched. It almost looked like a smile.

10

Pete

Lucas does not fuck around. You can say a lot of horrible shit about him and all of it would be true, but he absolutely *does not fuck around.* If he's ever caught, which I seriously doubt will happen, there is no question in my mind that he will rocket into the stratosphere of criminal celebrity. And in the unlikely case that he is taken alive, after an army of cops, reporters, jurors, psychiatrists, groupies, murder junkies, filmmakers, authors and musicians have gone public with who they think he is and what he means to them, he's gonna be the number one swinging-dick rock n' roll king of serial killers. In a world full of backpedaling dysfunctional why-me crybabies who talk a lot of shit and can't carry through on any of it, Lucas, as fucked up as it may seem for me to say it, is basically what every guy wants to be and every girl wants to spread for--a total animal who doesn't give a fuck for anything or anybody and does whatever he wants, whenever he feels like it, with no fear of consequence.

I looked up to him. You couldn't have gotten me to admit it under torture, but I did. I also hated his goddamn guts. If I thought about him for too long and with any kind of depth, he made me sick. The only emotions I ever saw him show in the three years I knew him were hate, bloodlust and contempt for anything and everything. It was impossible to like him, but I did. I couldn't help myself. Maybe it was his complete lack of any kind of need to be liked that did it, or it was because I was a part of my own theory and subconsciously wanted to be just like him.

The house he led us to was in the swanky part of Sororityville, a big white one with new siding and a bench swing hanging from chains on the open front porch. There were no Greek letters on the front of it; this wasn't an official soratory pad, it was a satellite house, where a bunch of rich girls who don't live in the real sorority house get drunk and share tampons and burn Ramen noodles. Sometimes they do it because there's no room in the main house, or they don't like their best friends who already live there, or the line for the curling iron is too long, or the soratory they belong to "officially" frowns on the recreational use of cocaine. At least those are the reasons I came up with after hours of being forced to listen to them talk to each other before and during classes.

It was a nice house, clean enough on the outside to belong

to somebody's parents. Our house, which looked like a cheap shithole to begin with, looked a hundred times worse by comparison.

"Rich bitches," Dave said. "I swear to crap, if the top of their stove is clean, I'm gonna be so pissed off."

Lucas took a pair of black leather gloves out of his back pocket and pulled them on. We could hear them inside, laughing and having some kind of good-natured argument. That was bad. The curtains were closed, and there was no way to tell how many of them were in there. It could have been two or twenty-two, for all we knew.

"I don't like it," I said. "It's too early."

Lucas tapped Dave's chest with the back of his hand. "Upstairs."

Dave finished pulling his own gloves on, and I hurried to get mine on. I was pissed off. "I'm telling you, it's too early. People are still out."

Lucas took a step closer to me, and I had to bend my neck back so that I was looking into his face and not his chest. "You're on the back door."

"Would you fucking listen?" I hissed. "This is no good. They're still up and running around in there."

"They're *gonna* be running," Dave said. He was grinning again, but there wasn't anything amusing in it.

Lucas stepped off the sidewalk into the yard and started around the side of the house with Dave on his heels. I could follow or be left behind. I followed.

Friedman is a mid-sized hick town. The locals think all Chicago kids are thugs and criminals, so they lock everything up extra tight; the college kids from Chicago think they more or less moved into *The Andy Griffith Show,* so they leave everything wide open. Even with the stories and warnings about the shit we'd been doing everywhere, we were still walking in and out of pretty much any house we wanted. Everybody thinks it can't happen to them, because they're lucky or there are always a bunch of people hanging around or maybe because they're just plain stupid.

The back door of the satellite house was closed but unlocked, and we went in like we owned the place. If it had been locked there wouldn't have been more than a two-second delay--the door and lock were so old Lucas could have shouldered it one time and splintered it out of the jamb.

Lucas never broke stride. He turned the knob, opened the door, and kept walking through the kitchen and into the living room with Dave five steps behind him. A girl in a t-shirt and sweatpants was on her way to the sink with a dirty plate and glass in her hand; she had paused and was looking back over her shoulder so she wouldn't miss out on whatever witty one-liners her gal-pals were cracking. Her head turned a second too late at the creak of the back door and Lucas had her. He slammed his open right hand up into the tender skin of her throat, just below the snakehead of her chin and jaw-line, and lifted her off her feet. The small of her back collided with the corner of the television and she dropped to the floor with it on top of her.

A brunette with shitty hair jumped out of the way and opened her mouth to scream; Lucas gave her a right hook that broke her jaw and dropped her like a bag of cement mix. The front door had a deadbolt and a chain on it, and he locked them both. The whole movement, from the time he turned the back door knob to the time he slid the front door chain, took less than thirty seconds.

I locked the back door. Dave grabbed a long bread knife off the counter—-it still had wet tomato sauce and coagulating cheese on it—-and ran up the stairs to the second floor. I started yanking drawers open, looking for a knife of my own. I felt like I was going to be sick, but good-sick, as if all my blood had been sucked out of my veins and replaced with low-voltage lightning.

People are strange when you scare the living hell out of them. You'd think the first thing a girl would do when she sees a complete stranger standing in her living room with obvious bad intentions is scream her head off. That's the way it happens on TV. The reality is that it takes them a few seconds to catch on to the situation. True fear makes voluntary bodily functions involuntary. They *want* to scream. Their mouths gob up and down, their eyes get wide and teary, their faces get pale. They tremble and shake. Sometimes they lose control of their bladders and piss all over the nice comfy furniture and shag carpeting. And no matter what they do, or what it looks like... It's beautiful. Absolutely stunning. Because it's real, as real as anything can ever get, and it can't be hidden and it can't be faked. The rush it gives you is like nothing else in the world.

But I wasn't getting any thrills at all, because I was still looking for a goddamn knife. The only prospects I found in the drawers were a claw hammer with a black rubber grip on the handle and some stainless steel shish-ke-bob skewers with rings on the ends of them. Finally I gave up on the drawers and started rummaging through the dirty shit in the sink.

You would think that girls are cleaner than guys. Not true. If anything, they're nastier. They'll eat half of something and throw the plate in the sink with the rest of the food still on it. These bitches were so lazy they'd started to wash their dishes, then quit and didn't even drain the water out, so I ended up jamming my hand into four inches of cold gray slop, which didn't do anything to help my mood. All I got out of the deal was a wet glove and a pathetic little paring knife that looked too dull to cut paper.

I tossed the hammer in Lucas' direction and he caught it by the head. By this time they'd started screaming and whimpering and crying, and they were jittering around, ready to run. None of them were hot-hot, but they were okay. One of them had a fat, bouncy pair of tits, but her ass was kind of big. I thought Lucas would do her first, because she was closest to him, but he grabbed her by the hair and threw her over the coffee table so that her elbows hit the floor and her knees and thighs were caught at an awkward angle that made it hard for her to get up.

There was a scream from upstairs, followed by the sound of Dave's laughter. A girl came down the whole set of stairs without her feet touching any of them and landed on her stomach. All her air came out in one gasp and she rolled over, choking on nothing and clutching at her throat as she tried to get it back. The towel she'd been wearing fell open and she was naked in front of us. Her crotch was hairless except for the perfect shape of a heart made of damp black curls.

I don't know what it was about it, but the sight of that heart made my dick so hard so fast, I thought I was gonna shoot off right there in my pants. I mean, I've been really turned on before, but that was fucking ridiculous. It was all I could do not to drop trou and jump on her.

Dave leapt from four steps up and landed on her perfect little belly with both feet, laughing as he lost his balance and banged his head on the corner of the open kitchen doorway. Heart Girl choked again; this time a thick spray of dark blood flew from her mouth and stained her lips and chin, and I knew something had burst. The sole-prints of Dave's Airwalks were already starting to welt up on the curve of her cute little belly.

I love it when a chick actually has a belly. I like really thin girls with nice tits--not huge, or even all that big, just nice--a narrow waist, and just a soft little curve in their stomachs. The whole six-pack rock hard abs thing is disgusting. Who in their right mind could look at a girl with a flat, lumpy stomach and find that appealing? To me, a sexy girl is firm, not hard. She shouldn't jiggle for two minutes after she's done laughing, but I like to see her body ripple back and forth a little bit when we're having sex. That's hot. Firm thighs too, and her hips set up so that when she stands naked with her back to you, you can see a little bit of light between her vagina and inner thighs, like a diamond.

I caught a flash of movement in my peripheral vision and turned just in time to see Lucas sink the hammer's claw into the forehead of another brunette. She'd thrown her hands up, like that was going to make some kind of difference, and he'd chopped the middle and ring fingers off her left hand. The hammer wouldn't come out of her head and he yanked and twisted it, planting his boot in her chest and prying at it until the bone behind her eyebrow gave and the skin stretched enough to give it back to him. Blood and brain fluid splattered everywhere.

The girl with the big chest had managed to get up and was going to make a break for the back door. I dove at her, slamming my shoulder into her pubic bone. Her head went over the top of me and she landed on my back. Her face bounced off the crack of my ass and she pounded the backs of my legs with her fists, screaming unintelligibly until Dave took a two-step start and kicked her right ear. She rolled off me and I stabbed her in the chest a few times with the paring knife until I could hear blood sucking into her lungs.

TV Girl had pried herself out from under the set and was working on the fake gold chain on the front door. Dave slammed into her from behind, pressing his chest into her back and stabbing her in the side once. He backed off and she staggered after him, the knife handle jutting out of the spreading black patch on her purple t-shirt like the throttle of a motorcycle. He backhanded her. She reached for the knife handle and let out a muted, sobbing shriek. The crotch of her orange sweatpants darkened with urine and she fell to her knees, trembling.

"Uhm-inh-ah," she said. "Off-nur-ope."

"Uh huh," Dave nodded, cocking his head to one side. "Go on."

"Grib... grib..." TV Girl said. Her fingers brushed against her wet crotch and she held them up for examination. She frowned at them, looked down at herself, saw the blood, and let out a weak, stuttering scream that sounded like somebody strangling a cat as heard through a shitty boombox.

"Yeah," Dave nodded. "That's what I was thinking. But the question that crossed my mind is, how long will it keep? Because it's gonna start to smell eventually, and I have no idea how to begin any kind of taxidermy procedure. And, even if I was a good taxidermist, I doubt the lips would keep the same texture and softness."

Lucas stopped beating the girl with shitty hair and a broken jaw in the face with the hammer and looked at Dave. His right eyebrow looked like it had raspberry jelly in it. "What?"

"We're discussing the possibility of me cutting her head off and taking it home with me," Dave said. "She's all for it, but I don't think I'm ready for that kind of commitment. I mean, I'm only 22."

"What the hell would you do with her head?" I said.

"You know, I could practice kissing on it and stuff. And I could use it for other things, but not until, you know, I'm done with the kissing."

"Wouldn't it be easier to just go pick up some slut at the bar?" I said. "That girl in your ceramics class thinks you're hot, you could just call her."

"Pete," he said, speaking very slowly, as if I were learning disabled in some way. "This girl is right here."

"Yeah, but she's dead," I said.

TV Girl blinked and let out a scratchy lowing sound.

"We've been friends for a long time, Pete. A long time. But I'm not going to let you bad-mouth Marcy. You'll just have to come to terms with the fact that she's in my life now, too."

"What the fuck are you even talking about?" I said. "And how do you know her name's Marcy?"

"Who gives a shit what her name is?" he snorted. "She's not gonna come when I call her anyway." He nudged at TV Girl with the toe of his sneaker. "Man, she's got endurance. I don't know if I could handle a chick like this. She'll probably get mad when I come in like 30 seconds and then just sit there on a pile of dirty laundry in the corner of my room, staring at me like the ass that I am. I don't need that kind of depression. And it's not like I can cut her tits off or anything to make myself feel better, because I won't have them anymore."

Any other time and I would have been laughing myself insane over that, but somehow it just made me feel sick. I didn't want to be there anymore. I was repulsed by all of us, me more than anybody. This was what I was and these were the things I did. I was a worthless, scum-sucking piece of shit. These chicks hadn't done anything to me. I'd never even seen them. And I'd helped to fuck them up so bad that most of their parents couldn't even have open-coffin funerals for them.

Heart Girl was what broke me. Not completely, maybe, but she sure put a crack in the foundation. Her crotch was exquisite. I had never seen anything more beautiful in my life. The puffy pout of her Venus mound, the delicate snake-tongue pink of her lips. She was stone dead now. Whatever Dave had done to her insides when he jumped on her had done more damage inside than out, because we'd all forgotten about her and nobody else had touched her. She was sprawled on the floor in front of the kitchen, one arm across her stomach so that the tips of her fingers just brushed the top of that perfect black heart.

Would she ever have gone out with me if we hadn't killed her? Possibly. I wasn't like Dave and Lucas. I had normal social skills, and good ones. I could have charmed her, maybe. She might have been into me.

So I'm shallow. Sue me. She was fucking hot. It almost made me wish I had Dave's sexual inclinations, because if there was any part of me that didn't find screwing a dead body totally repellent, I would have been right down there on her. She looked that good, dead or not. Thinking about it was freaking me out. I was almost in love with a corpse, and antsy, and I wanted to go. Preferably straight back to the house, so I could masturbate at least five times before I passed out from exhaustion, an aching wrist and a raw dick.

TV Girl was still on her knees, leaking fluid from two holes and swaying back and forth in some breeze none of the rest of us felt. She tried to swallow, but her tongue and throat were too thick and dry to get the job done and all that came out was a padded clicking sound. "I can't figure chicks out," Dave said thoughtfully.

"What's to figure out?" I asked.

"I have no idea."

11

Pete

Lucas had said he was out to do some damage, and we had done plenty by anybody's standards. Five girls, five bodies, and all of them in bad, bad shape. I was left on lookout again while he and Dave ransacked the upstairs. Rich girls always had jewelry and nice TVs and crap like that, but it was off-limits. Lucas wouldn't let us take it because if we got caught with it, it was a direct link between us and the crime. Sometimes we found photos and videotapes of chicks naked and fucking, which is always hot no matter what the chick looks like, but those were off-limits too. Dave and I tried talking him out of it when it came to the sex stuff, especially the time we found the video of a soratory chick going down on her little sister and sticking all sorts of weird shit in her--lollipops, a banana, lime green anal beads and a disgustingly huge dildo. No dice. We had to settle for leaving it on the chick's bed with a pile of framed citizenship awards we'd ripped off her walls and a sweatshirt that said *World's Best Sister!* We were still bummed out about it. The little sister couldn't have been more than 14, and we didn't even know an asshole could be stretched that wide. I bet it got swiped out of the evidence room and some wife-beating cop is still watching it with a bottle of Lubriderm three times a week.

The only things we took were money, drugs, and condoms. The money we split three ways. Lucas took the drugs, prescription stuff mostly, but illegal stuff if they had it. Pot, opium, speed, acid, mushrooms, shit like that. If there was any coke, crack, crystal meth or heroin, he left it, along with the syringes and kit, because we knew it would look bad when the cops found it and we were always curious to see if it got mentioned in the papers. It rarely did. Dave took the condoms because he found it embarrassing to go into a store and buy them and believed that they should be free.

They didn't find much in the satellite house, although Dave said one of the girls, probably Heart Girl, had some nice panties and a silver vibrator. When he'd finished turning off the last of the lights he knelt beside the girl with the big tits, pulled her shirt up, and let out a long low wolf-whistle. The streetlight in front of the house was bright, and if you didn't look too hard at the blood, you wouldn't even have known she was dead.

"You're really sick," I told him.

"You think?" he said.

"Yeah."

"Got any Pepto Bismol?"

"No."

He grabbed one of her brownish nipples and tugged on it. "Then shut the fuck up."

Lucas lit a cigarette and flicked the first ash onto what

was left of Broken Jaw's face. We looked at him.

"I think maybe that's a bad thing you're doing," I said.

"What do they care?" Dave said. "They're fucking dead. Plus, I like to think of us as bad people, and bad people do bad things. And you know what? This girl's a bad thing. Right? Get it? Like, I'm gonna do a bad thing. The girl. Bwa-ha."

"I'm talking about the cigarette, asshole. If he drops the butt, it's evidence."

Dave shook his head. "Christ you're paranoid."

"I'll be careful," Lucas said.

"You're a saint," I told him.

"Hey, don't breathe!" Dave said. "That's DNA evidence."

"You already left DNA, slobbering all over her tits," I muttered.

"What can I say? This bitch is hot."

"She's fucking dead! Her lips are blue!"

"I thought you liked that punk rock look," Lucas said.

"Shut up. Seriously, we should get out of here. We're gonna get nailed."

"I'd like to nail Jen number three," Dave said, staring at Heart Girl's crotch. "I think I messed her up too bad, though. If those aren't her guts sliding out of her cooter, she's got one hell of a yeast infection."

"Fucking disgusting," I said. I wish I hadn't looked at her again, because I think he was right. Those were definitely her guts sliding out of her cooter. It completely ruined Heart Girl for me. "That's totally like... necrophilia."

"Like?" Lucas said.

"Not really," Dave said.

"Pretty damn close," I said.

"It's not her neck he wants to touch," Lucas smirked.

Dave leaned over and whispered into Heart Girl's face. "Don't worry baby, you won't get pregnant. I like you."

Headlights hit the wall as a car pulled into the driveway out front, and we all froze. "Spread out," Lucas ordered. "We got a live one."

I jumped over Heart Girl and dragged her into the kitchen by her hair. A coat rack had been knocked over at some point; Dave took one of the coats and threw it over the face of the girl with the big tits. He took two more and held them up beside his face, standing in the spot where the rack had been, just inside the front door. They hid him from the top of his head to the middle of his stomach.

Lucas was nowhere in sight, but the fake gold chain was loose and still scraping back and forth against the jamb from when the doorknob rattled. The girl shut the door behind her and went upstairs without turning on the living room lights. We were okay for a minute or two, tops. Once she turned on a light and saw shit thrown every which way, things were going to go bad in a hurry.

I leaned out of the kitchen. "What the fuck are you doing?" I hissed.

"It's that slut from the other night!" Dave stage-whispered. "The one with the phone in the shitter!"

A light came on and I jumped back when I realized I could see the Crimson Ghost skull on my Misfits t-shirt. I waited for Phone Girl to scream and didn't hear anything.

"I thought you trashed the place," I said.

"One of the rooms was locked."

Sometimes you can't lose for winning. I tried to find Lucas again, but I couldn't do much without crossing through the patch of light coming from Phone Girl's open bedroom door, which didn't seem like such a hot idea. I'd been caught out once in a situation like this, and the bitch-- some jock cunt who was as strong as a fucking ox--almost choked me to death before Lucas stopped laughing and got her off me. That had been in the winter, so I could get away with wearing a scarf everywhere until the bruises on my throat faded out.

I wasn't taking any chances this time. Winter was a long way off.

12

Pete

Wherever Phone Girl was going, she was in a hurry. The light went off in her room and she shut and locked the door. This struck me as curious, because if you live in a house with your "best friends," why do you need to lock the door to your bedroom? Especially when they're all rich soratory cunts whose mommies and daddies would probably give them anything if they just made a phone call. I lived in a house with two bloodthirsty psychopaths and I never locked my door unless I was naked, either because I was jerking off or it was so hot I was sleeping in the raw. The only reasons I could come up with were that she either had something really, really scandalous in there that she didn't want anyone to find, or Dave and Lucas had been right in their opinions that frat and soratory kids were the worst kind of scum going, and even they knew it.

Anyway, Phone Girl came down the stairs fast and headed straight for the front door again without turning on the lights. It was dark in there, especially after being in a lit room the way she had, and you don't expect to trip over a dead body behind your own couch. But her foot caught the ankle of the chick with the big tits and the coat on her face, and Phone Girl hit the floor hard.

"Shit!" she said, and picked herself up. I could see her silhouette as my eyes began to adjust again, and she was headed for the light switch. Telepathy isn't one of my gifts, which was too bad for her. I thought at her as hard as I could, trying to shoot her a warning not to turn the lights on. I didn't want to do anymore of them that night. I was tired and horny and pissed off and sick of myself. If she just went out the front door and closed it behind her, I was 95% sure she'd live. Lucas wouldn't chase her outside.

But if you trip over something in the dark, the first thing you do is track down the nearest source of illumination and find out what it was. It's human nature, probably one of the only survival instincts we have leftover from the days when our ancestors lived in caves and had to worry about saber-toothed tigers and crabs the size of marbles crawling around in your treasure-trail if you got some action from the wrong cavegirl. So she turned on the lights. There was nothing else she could do. I gave her the loudest thought/scream/warning I had in me, and it just wasn't enough. When it's your time, it's your time, and you only get saved from that on television.

The lights blinded me when they came on, and her too, I think. Lucas was standing with his back against the front door. You couldn't see much of the door. It sent a jolt through me, and I've seen the big ugly bastard up close and personal enough times to get over shit like that. If he'd have leaned forward a little bit, he could have licked the tip of her nose. He exhaled a cloud of used smoke into her face and held up a kitchen knife. It wasn't one of the ones Dave and I had found. And I don't know where he got it, but it had been in somebody a few times.

Phone Girl opened her mouth to scream and Dave slapped one of the coats he was holding into her face. She screamed anyway, but it was nothing. Lucas stabbed her in the side with his left hand and punched her hard in the stomach with his right, and she was down. Then he flipped the lights off and blinded me again.

"I told you we should have gotten the fuck out of here 20 minutes ago, but you assholes had to stand around and give me shit," I said. "Real fucking funny. You guys are gonna laugh us right into jail."

Nobody listened to me, as usual. Dave had his bread knife out and was moving toward her, ready to finish the job with his usual good cheer. Lucas took another drag off his smoke; I could see the cherry wink in the dark, his top lip and the bottom of his nose flashing orange in the dark and then disappearing again. I didn't have to see him to know he was staring at me like I was an asshole.

A horn honked, and the three of us froze. Phone Girl groaned on the floor and I heard car doors slam. Lucas eased the drapes back with his fingers and looked out.

"Two more coming," he said. "Frat rats."

I came out of the kitchen doorway. "God-fucking-damn it!" I said. My voice was too loud but I didn't give a shit. "I knew this was gonna happen."

I saw Dave's shape straighten up and take a step back from Phone Girl. "Uh...?"

Lucas held his knife out to me, handle-first. "You two hit the first one as soon as he gets all the way in. I got number two."

I took the knife. It felt good in my hand, better than usual, because I was steaming. "Kill him?" I said, and felt like a jackass as soon as the words were out of my mouth.

"No. Sing him a fucking lullaby."

The amount of leeway a man in his 20's gets from his friends in the wake of a social gaffe, no matter how small, makes the image of hyenas scavenging a rotting, flyblown carcass seem cute and cuddly by comparison.

The front door opened and the first guy paused, trying to get his bearings in the dark. He was wearing a sling. "Katie? I gotta use the pisser." No answer. I found out later that Dave had been kneeling on the floor with his hand clamped over her mouth and a knife at her throat. The guy took three steps in. "Katie?"

The second fuckhead wasn't even in yet, but I was edgy and jumped the gun. Dave saw me moving and came up like a shot, and we hit him at the same time. I stuck my knife into his back and Dave got him in the stomach, so he was sandwiched between us. Any direction he tried to move he'd be sawing himself, which seemed like a good plan until I leaned too hard the wrong way and the blade of my knife snapped off halfway down. I fell across it and sliced a gash almost the length of my left forearm.

"Son of a *bitch!*" Dave said. Apparently my falling not only drove the guy into him--putting a nice bruise the exact shape and size of the butt of the knife handle in his chest-- but sent a thick spurt of my blood right into his face.

The second guy stepped through the door and saw me in the rectangle of outside light. "What the fuck--"

Lucas grabbed him by the throat, bashed his head against the doorjamb three times, then hooked an arm under his chin and yanked his head to the side with a crack that sounded like a fart under three blankets. He shoved the second guy into the room, off to the side and out of the way, and shut the door.

Dave had pulled his knife out of the first guy's guts and let him drop. "You okay?" he asked me.

"I think I cut my fucking arm off," I said. The cut was already burning, and it hadn't stopped gushing blood yet.

"He's alright," Lucas said. He turned the lights on again. "What about that piece of shit?"

Dave grabbed the first guy's bad arm and rolled him over. The guy was gasping—-a nasty, shallow, wet sound. "Hey, whatta you know?" Dave said. "It's Mr. I'm-Gonna-Kick-Some-Ass-Cause-That's-What-I-Do."

"Don't kill me," Boyfriend Mike from the restaurant said. "Don't fuckin' kill me, man. I won't... I won't tell nobody. Just don't--"

Dave was having none of it. I think that punch in the face bothered him more than he'd let on. "Hey, remember me? You hit me because you're an asshole, but then my friend kicked the shit out of you in front of all those people? Man, I never laughed so hard in my whole life. That look you got on your face, when you passed out for a second and then I was squirting ketchup all over your crotch? Classic!"

"Fucking waste him and let's go!" I said. "I'm bleeding to death over here."

Lucas grabbed what was left of the broken knife and held it out to me. "You fucked it up."

I backed away and shook my head. "I can't."

"Whatta you mean you can't?" Dave demanded. "If you're not gonna let me talk about old times with him, kill him and let's go. That's just rude."

"I'm fucking *bleeding* to death!" I said. I suppose I thought if I put the right inflection on it one of them would give a shit. Which just goes to show how intense pain can alter your grasp of reality.

Lucas jammed his free hand into my chest and sent me flying backwards. My heels hit the girl with the big tits and my ass hit the floor. The backs of my calves forced the last air out of her with a gassy *woosh*.

Lucas squatted down next to Boyfriend Mike and put the broken knife to his throat.

"I swear I won't say nothin'," Boyfriend Mike said. His

nose was broken and taped, his eyes black. When he opened his mouth I could see the holes where his teeth had been until Lucas knocked them out. "Just don't kill me. Please, man. *Please.*"

Lucas sliced both sides of his throat over the jugular veins and stuck the knife in his mouth like a tongue depressor. Then he picked me up and stood me on my feet.

"Damn," Dave said. The note of admiration in his voice was hard to miss. "What about the car? It's still--"

Phone Girl let out a guttural moan. We'd forgotten about her.

"Hey, ol' Shit-and-Shout isn't dead yet," Dave said. "That's not good."

Phone Girl staggered to her feet, and calling it a stagger is giving her the benefit of the doubt. She was in bad shape. Her hip hit an endtable and sent the lamp on top of it to the carpet. "Ugh..."

"Wise words from one of the true geniuses of the 21st century," Dave grinned. "Well well, long time no see, tits. Wear any good specials lately?"

Phone Girl squinted at him, at the knife in his hand, and promptly wet herself. We stood there for a minute, watching the front of her jeans get dark and listening to her pee splatter the carpet around her ankles.

"Now who's dirty, bitch?" Dave asked her. He dropped his knife, grabbed her by the hair, and bashed her head into the corner of the endtable until blood was flying every time he brought it up. She twitched and kicked for a good 90 seconds after his arm got tired and he dropped her.

79

My body was in a race to pass out or puke, and it was too close to call. "Not to be a whiner or anything--"

"Wonders never cease," Dave said.

The room was beginning to take on a gauzy look. "I am sort of fucking bleeding to death here," I sighed.

Lucas found a scarf on the floor and handed it to me. "Wrap it tight. It's a long walk home." He picked up the knife Dave had dropped and walked toward the kitchen. "Dave. Come here."

Dave went. "Look at that," Lucas said.

"What?"

"Your footprints on her stomach."

"I'm taking it that's not a good thing."

"Not for you. How many guys do you think are walking around with size 11 Airwalks?"

"A lot?"

"Not enough."

"So what do we do about that?"

I frowned with a face that seemed to weigh 40 lbs. and tried to loop the scarf around my arm as best I could. "I bet Ted Bundy didn't have to walk home with his arm cut off," I mumbled.

Something flat and rubbery flew out the kitchen door like a frisbee and landed in Boyfriend Mike's hair. I stared at it, trying to figure out what it was. There was a small silver hoop in it and I almost threw up when I realized it was the skin that had been covering Heart Girl's beautiful curvy stomach.

"Ted Bundy..." I said again.

Lucas plucked his spent cigarette butt off the floor beside Boyfriend Mike's leather sandal and dropped it in his chest pocket. "I heard you the first time," he said. He unwrapped the scarf on my arm and rewrapped it almost uncomfortably tight. "And if you don't quit crying and move your ass you're gonna get a chair just like his."

He and Dave looked at each other, grinned, and at the same time, *"Bzzzzzzzzzt!"*

Lucas rolled the patch of skin up like a poster and stuck it in his back pocket. When he dropped the tail of his shirt you couldn't even see it. All his clothes were big and baggy. We left.

13

<u>Dave</u>

So Pete was sitting on the toilet, swigging from a bottle of gin while Lucas stitched his arm with a needle and green thread. We tried to numb his arm with ice cubes, but he said that hurt and started being a whiny bitch about the whole thing. I was glad when he actually started saying that it hurt and articulating the words, because the constant grimacing and grinding of vocal chords that had proceeded the formation of those words were very cryptic clues, and I probably wouldn't have caught on otherwise. With the ice option no longer an option, we had to get him stupid-drunk in a hurry. He downed about half a bottle of gin in a time frame I'm too ashamed to mention, but if somebody just *had* to know, and threatened to stick a rolling pin up my ass, I'd tell them it was about as long as it took me to piss before he could sit down.

Why anyone would want to drink gin, I don't know. Vodka costs and looks the same, and it's right next to it on the shelf at the liquor store. Gin is a nice card game for people of all ages. Vodka sounds like a Russian expletive. Plus, vodka never tastes like a pine tree under any circumstances. But Lucas likes gin, and since he's usually the one who buys whatever I mooch, I end up having to drink it a lot.

Me, I was drinking a bottle of $2 wine, because I'm classy. Specifically, Boone's Farm Strawberry Daiquiri, which shares no real similarity whatsoever to a real daiquiri, unless you count the fact that it's red. But far be it from me to complain about anything that tastes like Hawaiian Punch and fucks you up for two bucks. Plus, like I said, I'm classy.

Our bathroom, which was usually as clean as a whistle that someone had dipped in mildew, now looked like The Fonz had just botched another motorcycle jump. "Is he gonna be ok?" I asked. Lucas ignored me and kept going grandma on Pete's ass. Where the hell an animal like him ever learned how to sew I'll never understand, but he was pretty good at it. One last tight little X, uncomfortably close to the faint blue Y of vein by Pete's wrist, and he bit the excess thread off, smearing blood all over his mouth.

"All done?" Pete giggled. His head kept rolling back, but now it was the booze causing his stupor and not the pain. Not that it was much of an improvement. After all, a stupor is a stupor. His face was almost as white as the toilet should have been, and coupled with his blood on Lucas' mouth, they looked like two clowns who were out of work for good reason.

Lucas said, "Take another pull. It's gonna sting," and grabbed a bottle of hydrogen peroxide off the back of the sink. Pete took a three-glugger that made him shudder, but he still licked his lips.

"I swear to crap they purposely make gin taste like nailpolish remover," he said, putting an accusing glare on the soon-to-be-empty bottle.

"You've tasted nailpolish remover?" I said.

"I got sisters."

"No wonder you're such a bitch." I took a swig of it and my entire head shook back and forth involuntarily. That crap was like liquid electroshock treatment every time I drank it. "Not nailpolish remover so much as... paint thinner."

"You tasted paint thinner?"

"I'm an artist." In reality I hadn't drawn much more than breath since high school, but I couldn't let him one-up me on my own joke. My own medicine tastes worse than gin. "Good thing you don't work in a sperm bank," Lucas said, filling in for the increasingly delirious Pete. He grabbed Pete's wrist and poured the peroxide on his arm. Pete grunted and tried to yank his arm back, which was entertaining. It looked like a gazelle trying to get out of the mouth of one of those big river crocodiles on the *Discovery Channel*. Pete was so smashed he didn't know what the hell he was doing, he just wanted his arm back. It was foaming red shit all over the place, and he kept screaming "Get it off! Get it off you piece of shit!" The guy must have had a good experience with gangrene sometime before I met him.

Lucas dropped the empty peroxide bottle into the sink and came out of the bathroom, wiping his hands on his jeans. The fresh red streaks it added to the drying patches already on there added a nice touch, I think. Crimson, brown and faded blue, very seventies. Pete staggered out behind him, clutching the gin bottle with one hand and the doorframe with the other. He handed the bottle to Lucas, who drained it and dropped it on top of the overflowing trashcan. The bottle rolled off onto the spreading disease carpet of Mountain Dew cans and used paper towels that had been accumulating since the last time we took the trash out.

"Is he gonna be ok?" I said. "Should we do something else?"

Lucas lit a cigarette. "Grab a mop."

Pete moaned. "God I feel shitty."

"Go watch TV," Lucas said. "I'll find you some painkillers." He took a six-pack of Pabst Blue Ribbon and a Ziploc bag of pills out of the fridge. From the Mystery Fun Bag, Pete won two chalky white magic beans that looked to be about twice the diameter of the human esophagus. The three "B's" of life with Lucas: bleeding, booze and barbiturates. Pete's post-op looked more dangerous than the affliction that had landed him in our back-alley abortion clinic of a hospital in the first place. I wondered if the HMO Lucas worked for knew about his malpractice.

"That's it? Aren't you gonna do anything else?" I said.

Lucas set the edge of a Pabst bottle cap on the counter and slammed it with the heel of his hand. The cap shot off and dropped into the pile of dirty dishes in the sink, and foam erupted from the top of the bottle. You had to hand it to the guy--he wasn't without talent. He sucked the froth up and barely spilled a drop. "Watch TV."

"How come I gotta clean this shit up and you get to watch TV?"

"That's what you get for not learning how to sew,

Betsy Ross. Some get old glory, some get to clean up the scraps."

"God fuck America." I grabbed the mop and looked at it. "Wait a minute, where the fuck did we get a mop?"

"I think it's Pete's."

"Uh-uh," Pete said. I think almost-dying improved his debating skills tenfold.

"Well fuck," I concluded, turning on the shower to wet the head. I took another look at the mess, dropped the mop, and turned the shower nozzle directly onto the floor.

14

Pete

My arm hurt like a bitch, but I had to hand it to Lucas--I couldn't have gotten better stitches in a hospital. The green thread was kind of lame, but his work was tight. He even showed me how to clean it with peroxide and put a baking soda paste on it when I went to bed at night that would make it heal faster. At first I thought he was jerking my cage about the baking soda, but it turned out to be good stuff. It kept the itching down for one thing, which helped me not to pull the stitches out by accident.

After I woke up and my head cleared from the cocktail of gin and pills Lucas had fed me, I started wondering what he'd done with Heart Girl's stomach. It wasn't the kind of thing you just threw out with the usual household trash, and I couldn't remember him ditching it anywhere on the way home. Knowing Lucas and his penchant for wearing the same jeans for a week or two without washing them, it was entirely possible he'd forgotten about it and his back pocket was holding more than just his wallet.

I couldn't think of a good way to broach the subject, and Lucas doesn't like small talk anyway. He's a good listener as long as there's a point being made or some sort of information being passed around that he can make productive use of later. Talking just for the sake of talking tends to irritate the shit out of him.

"Hey," I said, and slapped my own stomach so he'd know what I was talking about. "What did you do with that?"

"Gave it to Dave."

"Oh Jesus," I said. "Why?"

"He wanted it."

"For what?"

"He wanted me to sew him a wallet out of it or make a little drum or something."

"Holy shit," I groaned. "Tell me you didn't."

"No," Lucas said. He drained his bottle of Pabst Blue

Ribbon and went to the kitchen for another one. "That wallet idea wasn't bad, though."

"What?"

"With that belly button ring in there, it wouldn't have been hard to put a chain on it."

Living with a complete fucking psychopath had never bothered me much for some reason, but that day it was catching up with me in spades. I had always known Lucas was a lost cause, but Dave had never shown any real signs of the kind of degeneracy he was now displaying on a regular basis. With Lucas, no depraved, taboo idea was turned away unembraced, and the absolute acceptance of any ghastly thing under the sun had inspired Dave to come up with and try anything that might be over Lucas' line, wherever it was. Dave had been pushing buttons and boundaries in one way or another since we were in grade school together. Now that Lucas had destroyed them, it seemed to me as if Dave's sole purpose in life had become finding out exactly how deep the proverbial bottomless pit actually was.

"I can't believe you gave it to him," I said. "What if he gets caught with it?"

"We're getting rid of it today."

"How?"

"I don't know. Cut it up and burn it, probably. Throw the ashes in the fish pond." He came back into the living room and kicked a path through pieces of broken telephone so he could get to the TV and turn it over to HBO, where they were playing *The Cable Guy* again. We'd moved into the house in August. It was now the fourth week of September, and we'd already gone through nine phones. For some reason he and Dave kept smashing them, and they never cleaned the pieces up. I'd brought one from home, Dave brought one, and we found one in the endtable when we moved in. The rest of them were the shit-brown phones they issued, one to a room when you moved into the dorm. I didn't know where the two of them kept getting new ones all the time, and I didn't ask.

"Why did Dave want it?" I said. "What could he possibly do with it?"

Lucas just looked at me and waited for me to draw my own conclusions, all of which were sexual and none of which I ever wanted to draw again. Dave had once said something about inventing a condom that could be re-used, thereby sticking it to the Trojan corporation and avoiding the trauma of admitting that you didn't need the Magnum variety when you bought them in public.

For the first time ever, I wanted to punch Dave in the face. Just go to his room, kick the door in, and beat the living shit out of him. The best part of the hottest girl I had ever seen in my life, and he was doing God knows what with it. Too much was too goddamn much, and this was it.

"Relax," Lucas said around the Winston Light in his mouth as he lit it. "It'll pass."

"What will pass?"

"Don't get all riled up and do something you'll regret." He handed me his untouched beer and got up for another.

"I regret a lot of shit I've done, but I doubt what I'm

thinking about doing now will make the list," I said, and took a pull off the bottle. Ugh. Pabst is old man beer, and disgusting old man beer at that. Lucas drank it up like a little kid drinks Kool-Aid. Not that that's any great credit to it. I've seen Lucas drink Falstaff, Schlitz Ice, and some shit of his own invention called a Redrum--like from *The Shining*--which was made from bong water, cherry NyQuil, frozen vodka and water he'd boiled morning glory seeds in. The man was not exactly a connoisseur of fine beverages.

"You're horny," Lucas told me. "It'll work itself out."

"Are we talking about the same thing?" I said, and took another hork from the brown bottle of cirrhosis he'd given me. Man, that shit was tough. I needed something to dull my tastebuds. "Give me a cigarette."

He tossed me one. "That girl was cute. Your type, too. I saw you checking her out."

"She was magnificent," I said. "And I don't throw that word around like I own it."

"It'll pass," he said again.

"How do you know?"

"Give it enough time, everything passes."

"What a stunning life I lead," I said. The beer was starting to lose some of its bitterness. I wasn't. "Sitting in a shithole house drinking old man beer that tastes like bull piss, talking about matters of love and sex with a guy who's never had anything to do with either one, that I've seen. And this while he tries to convince me not to knock out my best friend's lights, because said best friend is probably getting off, as we speak, on the stomach of the hottest girl I have ever seen. Not the whole girl. Just the stomach."

The corner of Lucas' mouth went up. "Boo-fucking-hoo, hondo. If I stick a quarter up your ass, will you sing me another one?"

"Fuck you," I said. "I mean it. *Fuck. You.*"

"Man, you are horny."

I swore to myself right then and there that if I ever had the opportunity to attack Lucas and seriously hurt him, I would take it, no matter what it cost. What a fucking prick. And the worst part about talking to him was that you could never be sure if he was operating under his own warped notion of reality or just needling you for his own amusement.

"I'm really starting to get sick of you," I told him. "You can take that however you want."

He lit a cigarette. "I'll leave it."

We watched *The Cable Guy* for a while and drank some more beer. After the third one I couldn't really taste it anymore and the buzz started to kick in. Missing classes for the day didn't seem like such a big deal. Eventually Dave came upstairs, paused in the doorway and gave us both one of his patented rock-star points of acknowledgement.

"You guys are drinking already?" he said. "Fucking awesome. It's not even noon yet." He got one of Lucas' beers, copped a cigarette from him, and flopped down on the couch beside me.

"What the fuck did you do with that stomach?" I said.

He snorted and sprayed beer out his nose, which made him laugh even harder. He does that a lot, this nostril-spraying, and it's 100% genuine. Usually it's also highly amusing. "Is there any context in which that statement wouldn't hold comedic value?" he said.

Lucas shrugged.

"I'm serious," I said. "What did you do with it?"

"Used it to jerk off."

"Jesus Christ," I said. "That's disgusting."

"Scratchy too," he nodded. "It was better after I washed the dried blood off it and rubbed some lotion into it. You could feel all the little hairs and stuff. It was awesome."

"I think I'm gonna throw up."

"That ring in her bellybutton was kind of a pain in the ass, until I figured out which way to rub it," he said, and he was serious. "Overall, as masturbation experiences go, I'd give it five out of five stars. I was up and ready again in no time."

"How many times?" Lucas asked.

"Uh, three."

"Impressive."

"Yeah, I might do it some more, but I pulled out too late last time, so I'm gonna have to wash it again. I was gonna do it right after, but like, I got all sleepy and forgot."

"That chick was so fucking hot, it's killing me," I groaned.

"You want that thing?" Dave said. "I'll wash it off a rub some more lotion in it, it'll be good as new."

I charley-horsed his arm as hard as I could. He yelled and jumped, and his beer hit the carpet. Lucas leaned over and picked it up before most of it soaked in.

"Goddamn it, why are you hitting me?" Dave laughed.

He rubbed his bicep and winced. "That's not the sign of a true friend, Pete."

"I can't believe you fucked that thing," I said. The shitty old man beer was starting to go to my head. I was feeling loose and full of juice. "That's fucking pathetic!"

"No," he laughed, still rubbing his arm. "It was her stomach. I think Lucas left her pathetic intact. Isn't that near the kidneys?"

I punched him again, this time in the chest. He leaned over on the arm of the couch and curled up in a ball, still laughing. "Fuck! I told you I'd wash it for you, asshole!"

I stood up and drew back again. I was going to beat him until he quit laughing and then hit him a couple more times for good measure.

Lucas snapped a bottle cap at me that grazed off my stitches. It hurt like hell. "Hit him again, I snap your neck."

He was ten inches taller than me, outweighed me by at least 125 pounds. He was stronger than I would ever live to be and meaner than I could begin to imagine. Logic like that is hard to argue with. He didn't even have to raise his voice or put any kind of inflection in it. I believed him.

"You're a bitch," Dave groaned. He was still laughing, the prick. "Seriously. What a fucking pussy. You're lucky he stopped you before I went Bill Bixby on you and ripped my shirt. Then I would have really been pissed."

I jacked him in the knee and fell back on the couch, shaking my hand. He, of course, laughed even harder. If I couldn't beat him into submission, the best I could hope for was to make him laugh his stupid self to death.

"What's your problem?" he said, when he got enough air back to speak. "Are you really that pissed off about it?"

"Yeah," I said. "No. I don't know."

"Well, at least you're still decisive," Dave said. Lucas gave him back his beer; he chugged half of it and put the bottle against his bicep. "Man, you hit hard for a chick."

"I don't think," I said, "that I want to do this anymore."

They didn't say anything. Lucas finally got around to looking at me after Jim Carrey was finished slamming himself into an apartment door.

"I've had it," I said. "This isn't fun anymore."

Dave remembered his cigarette and plucked it off the floor, toeing the smoking hole in the stained brown carpet until it stopped. He poured some beer on the hole to make sure it was out and looked at me again. "Why not?"

"Something took it out of me," I said. I looked at Lucas. "Maybe it was that chick, I don't know. Those pills you gave me last night fucked my shit up bad. I was laying there watching the TV spin around and melt and whatever the hell else it was doing, and I just decided I've had enough."

Lucas got himself another beer. I was almost excited, in a weird way. I didn't know if this was going to be my final position on the subject, but it was out in the open, half-formed or not, which meant the guilt and anxiety of letting it roll around in my head and guts was automatically gone. And if anybody in the world could understand the weight of a life-decision made under the influence, it was Lucas. Dave and I looked at him, waiting for him to say something that would set all of this to rights.

Lucas lit another cigarette and began to clip his fingernails. We watched him do his right hand, thumb to pinky. Then we watched him go over them all again, making sure he hadn't left any sharp points or ragged edges. Then he did his hangnails. Then he collected all the little fingernail chips from his lap and the front of his shirt and dropped them on top of the mountain of spent butts in the ashtray.

When he started on his left hand, Dave cackled and shook his head. We'd been had. Lucas wasn't going to say anything unless you dragged it out of him with a motorized winch.

"Well?" I said.

"Well what?"

"Don't you have anything to say about it?"

"Quit," he shrugged. "I don't give a fuck."

Dave clamped his hand over his mouth and tried not to laugh again, kicking his heels against the bottom of the couch. His face was red and his eyes were beginning to water behind his glasses.

"That's it?" I said.

Lucas looked at me. "Pete, I really wish you wouldn't quit. You're a vital part of the team. You'd be doing all of us a real disservice by giving up at this point, maybe yourself more than anybody. I doubt we can win the big game against Rileyville this weekend without you, what with morale being so low after you turn your equipment in, and that'll be a real disappointment to the boys. You know how they hate those sonsabitches from Rileyville. Hell, it'll be a rough thing for the whole town. They're gonna feel let down, real let down. But if you've looked into your heart and had a talk with God, and this is really what you want to do, nobody on this team is gonna stand in your way. We'll just have to dig a little deeper, pull up our jocks, and try to do it without you. This is the game, son. Players come and players go, but the game waits for no one."

He held the bottle up to his mouth, which for once was grinning on both sides. "Something like that?" he said, and guzzled.

"Fuck you," I told him. "Fuck the both of you."

"I still love you Pete," Dave said, and went into another fit.

I slammed the front door behind me on the way out, but I could still hear him laughing.

15

Pete

Somehow--I'm not exactly clear on the circumstances, probably due to an after-effect of the massive doses of God-knows-what Lucas fed me after I got cut--I ended up wanting to go to the record store at the same time Dave and Lucas were going to the square, so I caught a ride with them. Lucas was the only one of us that had a car; I had to leave mine at home for my sister to use and Dave never got his license because he's afraid to drive. Plus it's easier for him to mooch a ride off of somebody else than to deal with insurance and tickets and buying gas and all the other stuff that goes with that particular cornerstone of the American Dream.

Lucas' car was a total white trash hot-rod, a 1981 Camaro that he'd jacked up in the back and outfitted with 17-inch rear tires, almost racing slicks but with just a little more tread on them. It was midnight blue, but the paint was starting to blister and scab on the hood and roof, and in a few spots on the front end you could see baby-blue peeking through where it had flaked off the fiberglass. It was a tough looking car. He did all the work on it himself, and kept it running like new, maybe better. We timed it once at 127 mph and he still had some give left in the accelerator, but it was three in the morning and he killed the headlights, and Dave and I freaked out and made him slow it down.

He didn't drive like a maniac very often, and never through town, but I still hated riding with him, because his taste in music sucked. Every time you got in that damn car he had some butt-rock crap cranked up, Ratt and Mötley Crüe and Cinderella and Twisted Sister, that kind of shit. There was an amplifier behind the backseat, where I always had to sit because Dave was always the first one to call out "I wanna suck your dick," which for some reason had replaced "shotgun" in our vernacular, and it was so loud it made my head hurt.

And, whenever we were in the car, there was always a version of the same conversation:

Dave: We should listen to something else.
Lucas: No we shouldn't.

Dave: Yeah, cause this stuff sucks. We should listen to the Pixies, or Nine Inch Nails.
Me: I hate Nine Inch Nails.
Dave: Seriously, we should listen to something else.
Lucas: No.
Dave: Why not?
Lucas: Because fuck you.
Dave: I know what you're trying to do, and it's not going to work. You're not going to trick me into liking this. (reaches for the tape deck)
Lucas: I could trick your nose into bleeding all over your shirt.
Dave: (hand frozen over volume knob) Is that better or worse than the bleeding I already have in my ears from listening to this crap?
Lucas: It'll be easy to compare. You'll have both.
Dave: (pulling hand back) Hard to argue with that logic.

So anyway, we found a parking spot on the square and piled out of the car. "I'm going to the record store," I said.

"We gotta go look at that stuff," Dave told me.

"You go look," I said. I didn't know what they were up to, but I was sure I didn't want anything to do with it. "I'm going to the record store."

"Yeah, cause you know what?" Dave said. "The fucking record store isn't still going to be open when we get done, asshole."

"I gotta get this new CD that comes out today before they're all gone," I told him.

"Yeah, I heard that new Ace of Bass album is supposed to kick ass," he grinned.

"Fuck that," I said. "I ain't buying no Ace of Bass album."

Then, those two assholes, they looked at each other and grinned, and started singing in a bad falsetto right there on the street *"All that Pete wants, is another baby--"*

"Screw you guys," I said, flipped them the bird, and took off.

16

Dave

So me and Lucas walk into this shop, one of those weird townie-owned stores without a memorable name or discernable focus or theme in their line of goods. This was one of the few stores in the square where we hadn't memorized every single item of merchandise, so although there's not a damn thing we'd ever want to buy there, it's still more interesting than a record store the size of a Burger King bathroom with 3 CDs you might buy if you didn't already own them. Actually, this particular place had a lot of metal shit. We stopped to examine a glass case of brutal-looking knives, for obvious purposes, and I held my breath in hopes that I might be able to hear Lucas getting erect inside his jeans, thereby proving another of my theories correct. I'm not fucking gay, though.

There was some sort of crappy employer/employee conflict at the front of the store. The manager stroke--he had a moustache, dead giveaway--this pudgy guy who looked like the slightest annoyance might send him into a massive coronary, was standing by the jewelry counter yelling at the salesgirl. She was polishing her ring with a bored expression. I would be too.

"Where's Rachel?" he growled, like Clint Eastwood might if he was fat, had a mustache and hemorrhoids and ran a crappy store in a crappy college town. "I told her to rearrange the friendship bracelet displays a half hour ago!"

"I don't know. I think she was gonna like, do something in the back, or something," articulated the salesgirl. If you could call her a salesgirl, or articulate.

"Goddamn it, when I tell you girls to do something, I want it done now, not at your earliest convenience!"

Salesgirl just stared at him like the asshole he was. He looked out the front window and started rapping on it with his knuckles and pointed at the floor like he was calling a dog. There was a girl standing out there smoking, she rolled her eyes and tossed the cigarette into the gutter and came in.

Mr. Moustache was livid. "Rachel! I'm paying you to work and you stand around smoking? You're fired! Get out of my store and don't come back!"

The Rachel chick smiled sweetly at Lucas and me, tucked a lock of hair behind her ear, then planted both hands in his chest and shoved him backward into the display case of earrings, which exploded like a Vietnam frag mine in some movie where people cuss a lot and smoke pot.

"Fuck you and your store, you piece of shit," she said.

"Wow," I said to Lucas. "Physical confrontation and she's not even screaming at him."

Mr. Moustache steadied himself on the counter, looking like a girl had just shoved him into a display case in his own store. There's not much else you can look like after something like that. His face turned red and wet. "I said you're fired! Now get the hell out!"

"You can keep your stupid job," the violent chick said. "At least now I won't have to worry about you raping me with your eyes every time I bend over."

Mr. Mustache looked anxiously at us, worried that he could be losing potential customers. Too bad for him we wouldn't have bought anything anyways, because we refuse to support people with moustaches on general principle. "I don't know what you're talking about," he said. "Get the hell out of my store."

Why do old guys always say *hell* a lot when they're trying to be tough and serious? I mean, seriously, does the word *hell* really carry any weight with anybody anymore? And it could have been the fluorescent lights playing tricks with me, but I swear his eyes were welling up with tears in the third trimester. There's nothing more pathetic than seeing an old guy start boo-hooing right after he tries to have authority, unless it's watching Pete try to come up with reasons why I shouldn't eat his food.

"Your store, your store. Here's what I think of you and your rip-off store," the violent chick said, and she knocked another rack of earrings to the floor, scattering them everywhere, then shoved out the door and made one of those stupid bell-strips jingle like generic Christmas.

Mr. Moustache grunted, lowered himself to his knees and

started to clean up the mess. As we walked past him, I said "In case you were wondering, yes, that did escalate into a 'scene.'"

"Hey, I'm sorry about this fellas," he smiled. "I hope you'll come back and see us again when things are a little more calm."

I snorted. "Fuck you, eye-raper."

I'd probably eye-rape her too, but that's okay, because I'm not her boss, right?

So we leave to go meet Pete at the record store. When he steps out of it, the violent chick walks right into him, making him drop his new CD. "Watch where you're going!" she says. "Dick."

"I think I'm in love," I said. Nothing better than an over-assertive chick, especially when she's in the wrong.

Pete stomped over to us with an indignant look on his face. "Did you see that?" he said. "What a bitch."

"You're just mad cause she kicked your ass," I tell him.

"Maybe I oughtta kick *your* ass."

"You hear that?" I asked Lucas. "This kid's gay, he says he wants to kiss my ass."

"Kick! I said I'm gonna *kick* your ass!"

"Sure you did. Homo."

"Goddamn it."

"How's that new Ace of Bass CD?"

"I didn't buy Ace of Bass!" Pete yelled. His face started turning red under his little blond mustache and beard and he stomped off toward the car like a little bitch, so I won the fight.

17

<u>Dave</u>

So later I fell asleep reading *The Stand*, which I took from Lucas' room. It's 1000-plus pages, which is good, because the thicker a book is, the better I feel when I get bored and throw it at the wall. I had missed my Ceramics class again, which I might not have actually been in anymore since they automatically drop you from classes if you don't show up for the first two weeks. Ceramics is for anal-expulsive personalities anyway, people who get potty-trained too late in their babyhood so they spend their lives playing with substitute poopy. Pete was awesome at it. I'm pretty sure he was actually majoring in Ceramics, although I have no idea why. If you offered me a Ph.D. in Ceramics or a KFC coupon for $3.00 off, I'd go for the coupon. At least then I could feel relatively safe licking my fingers.

I got up and went to the kitchen for what might have been lunch, dinner, or both. I'd barely made a dent in the 40 packages of Ramen my mom had sent me the month before, so I grabbed a chicken flavor, which tasted like beef flavor, which tasted like oriental flavor, which tasted like the pot we hadn't washed in a month.

Pete was standing in the corner of the living room making his yo-yo fuck the dog or whatever, and Lucas was watching the news in his chair, munching a couple of Rolaids. The way that guy chews antacids, you'd swear he drinks molten lava with curry sprinkled on it 24 hours a day. The local perky blonde anchorwoman was behind the news desk smiling like she'd just put in a Prozac tampon, as usual.

"Our top story--a Chicago-area woman has taken on a one-woman crusade to catch a killer. Cynthia Dawson, sister of murder victim Katherine Dawson, has pledged that she will not return home until her sister's killer is brought to justice."

"What the fuck is this?" I asked, cranked on a burner on our once-white, now-orange, stove-top and walked into the living room.

"Dawson, a mother of two who worked as an investigative assistant with the Chicago Police Department for three years before leaving to become a homemaker, has offered her help to Friedman police, who by their own admission have yet to come up with any substantial leads."

They cut to a clip of Mrs. Cynthia Dawson, would-be soccer-mom, trophy wife and career bitch, who was sitting on a soundstage trying to look like she meant business without resorting to an expression of extreme cuntiness. Her voice was as tasteless as her hairstyle. "I don't claim to be an investigator by any stretch of the imagination. But I feel I'm in a position to help the police catch the murderer who took my sister from me, and I won't rest until he's brought to justice."

They showed a picture of her precious sister, and who do you think it was? *Phone Girl*. Just looking at her picture made me want to stab somebody, that bitch.

They cut back to the anchor-slut. "Dawson feels that someone may have a clue as to the killer's identity, although no one has come forward as of yet."

Back to Cindy Homemaker. "Someone out there knows something. Maybe they're afraid to come forward, maybe they don't want to turn in a friend or a loved one. But my sister has been taken from me, from our parents, from her friends and loved ones, and from the world. I ask you, if you know *anything, please* come forward so no one else has

to live through this kind of tragedy. The sooner we get this piece of trash off the streets, the sooner we can all sleep a little more soundly at night."

"I feel horrible," I announced. "I took something

from *the world.* You know what would make me sleep better? A law that nobody with an I.Q. under 70 would be allowed to take up valuable space on my fucking TV."

"A housewife?" Pete said. "Kirk Cameron's mom is

gonna come down here and catch us? What's she gonna do, beat us with a vacuum cleaner?"

It was time, once again, for one of our great debates, like JFK and Nixon, but without all the ties and sweating. And it was in color.

"What are you worried about, shorty?" I say. "She'll probably mistake you for a baby and slap a diaper on you."

"I'd rather be attacked with the vacuum," Pete says. "I rash easy."

"It probably wouldn't be that bad," I offer. "She might powder your tush, even use some of those baby wipes. I bet you'd get into it, and end up scheduling to have it done again."

"Next time we go out I think I'm gonna kill you by

mistake," Pete says.

That's funny, but I can't tell if he's kidding or not. "Go ahead and try it Gacy," I tell him. "Then we can watch you cut your other arm off."

Lucas actually laughed at that one.

"Besides," I say, "you just want to kill me so you can have sex with me."

"You're the fucking necro."

"It's odd that you would pick that for a defense," I tell him.

"Well seeing as how it should be obvious even to a

retard like yourself that I'm a manly heterosexual man, denying that I'm gay would only be redundant, wouldn't it?"

I'm almost stumped. "But if given a choice, would you rather have sex with a live man than a dead chick?"

"I wouldn't do either of them!" he yells. "Why the hell would I ever be put in a position where I would have to make that choice?"

Almost stumped again. Either I was having an off-night, or our boy Petey the Pirate was learning something. "I don't know how you get yourself into weird ultimatums like that, but you drive a hard bargain. What about a dead gay man?"

"I'm not fucking any dead people, and I'm not fucking any guys."

Now I could play the equal rights card. "That's discrimination. Homosexuals and the recently deceased have the same right to a good lay as the rest of us. I'm really disappointed in you, Pete."

"The way I see it, I'm not a 'good lay' anyways, so the homosexual and recently-deceased minorities you so champion would be better off not engaging in coitus with me anyhow."

He had a point.

"You're a better man than I thought," I say, and decide to call it a tie. I turned to Lucas, who changed the channel. "What are you thinking about?"

"How much I'd like to track down that bitch's house and gut her fucking kids in front of her."

Petey the Pirate almost dropped his gallon jug of orange Hi-C all over the poop deck, also known as the living room rug, which was covered with shit-brown carpeting, so it wasn't hard to make the connection. "Jesus Christ!" he said. "That's horrible! You wouldn't really do that, would you?"

Lucas, as usual, kept watching TV and didn't say anything. "Don't worry, you bleeding heart liberal," I said. "If I'm with him, I'll make sure to read them a bedtime story while he does it."

Pete stared at me. "Dave," he said. "That whole being casually bloodthirsty and tough thing? It works a lot better when he does it."

"Who gives a crap about that?" I said. "I just like bedtime stories. There's a lot to be learned from the *Clifford the Big Red Dog.*"

"Like what?"

"Sex," I said, because it was the first thing that came to mind, because I'm a guy and therefore only have two feelings--horny and more horny. "Everything I learned about sex, I learned from *Clifford the Big Red Dog."*

"Which would explain why you know nothing."

"You want to fight me, don't you?" I said.

"To the death."

"How about if we just thumb-wrestle until one of us is dyslexic?"

Pete got off the couch and started limbering up. "I'm totally gonna kick your ass. I rule at thumb-wrestling. If thumb-wrestling was an organized sport, I would be regional champ."

I did some squats and a few toe-touches and cracked my knuckles, which always hurts and never lets off those good pops like Lucas gets out of his. Then again, my fingers aren't crooked and don't have permanently swollen knuckles from beating people in the face like his do, either. "When I get done with you, you're gonna be the regional *chump*," I told him. "I'm gonna make you cry like a bitch. And I'm calling no figure-four leglocks this time."

"You can't call that."

"I just did. And I'm calling no leg-humps."

"You're the only one that does that!"

"Lucas," I said. "You're referee."

"Okay."

I saw Pete sniffing the air, and it occurred to me that I'd forgotten to take the Ramen off the stove, which explained the smoke billowing out of the kitchen. That cheap crap had not only burned black but melded to the inside of the pan. Now everything we cooked in it was going to taste like cheap Chinese charcoal.

"Isn't that one of my pans?" Pete said, when we got the fire put out.

"It used to be," I told him. "I think it's God's pan now."

18

Pete

A week passed, and nothing else was said about me quitting, by any of us. No one said much of anything at all when I was around. From Lucas you expected that, but I got the feeling that Dave was turning his back on me. He'd answer if I asked him a question, but it was just an answer. No jokes. After being used to the old Dave for twelve years, a Dave without jokes was depressing.

I stayed down in my room playing Super Nintendo with the door open, hoping they'd come in and want to start a tournament. My room was in the corner of the basement farthest away from the stairs, and neither of them walked past the door. Dave went to Lucas' room next door a few times; I could hear them laughing about something through the thin wall that separated his room and mine. Dave even did his laundry on our coin-operated machines in one five-hour marathon session, and for once he didn't ask me for quarters. But neither of them ever even looked in. The only times I saw them were when I went to the kitchen to get something to eat. Dave even stopped eating my food.

I tried to kill time by doing stuff I hadn't gotten around to doing for a long time, like going over to the dorm and checking my mail and the messages on my answering machine. My mom didn't want me living in a house--especially not with Dave, who she thought was the anti-Christ. As far as she was concerned I lived in 517 Corbin Hall. The bed had blankets on it, and I went over there from time to time to water my plants and do my Art assignments and other homework without distractions, but I almost never slept there. Sometimes Dave and I went over in the middle of the night to use the 24-hour computer lab in the basement and grab what passed for a hot meal in the cafeteria, which we paid for with my food card. Once when our water got shut off all of us went over there to use the showers until we got the money to turn it back on. The set-up had its advantages. It was also a good place to steal toilet paper, even if it was the generic kind that did more to tear your butthole off your body than to clean you up.

Moving into the dorm on a permanent basis was an option I started to seriously consider. If Dave and Lucas were going to be dicks to me, the hassles of living with them and their concepts of cleanliness and common courtesy weren't something I wanted to put up with anymore. It was still early enough in the year to find other people to hang out with, although the prospect of that didn't thrill me much either.

In college your friends are more or less a family that you actually like, and you get used to them. They're comfortable. Hanging out with Dave and Lucas non-stop for two years meant that I didn't really know anybody else, and anybody new I happened to meet was automatically a third-class human being. More of Lucas' misanthropy had rubbed off on me than I liked to admit. I still didn't believe he was right, exactly, but it was hard to dispute his arguments. There were too many and they were too well thought out. Playing devil's advocate with him was pointless--he had an answer for everything and could twist your own words almost before you got them out of your mouth.

And, as Dave often said to me, it was possible that Lucas *was* the devil. With Dave everything was a joke and everything wasn't, so I could never be sure if he was kidding or not. Neither was he, probably. It's not like Lucas was giving us any proof that he *wasn't* the devil.

As the week crept by I kept myself busy with classes and stupid little crap that I'd been putting off for too long. Organizing my CDs, reading the extra materials for some of my classes in the library, cleaning my room, re-potting my plants. I got a lot done, actually. But the more I tried not to think about things, the more I did. I didn't know how it would play out the next time I saw Dave and Lucas heading out the door with that extra shot of purpose in their strides. It was easy to tell myself I was done with it when nothing was going on, but sticking to what passed for my convictions in the heat of the moment was another thing altogether.

I drove myself nuts over it for a week and a day. Then came the moment of truth. I could hear them pacing the house like the caged animals they were, working their anticipation down to a level where they were sure they could think clearly and make no mistakes.

Anybody who's ever spent anytime around a budding

alcoholic knows that feeling in the air, right before the alkie-to-be heads out to the bar for the night. Pure tension, so thick you can taste it on the back of your tongue. I didn't need to be in the room with them; the creaking of the floorboards was enough to flip that switch in my brain, get me nervous and excited, make my skin feel like it was crawling around on itself with feathered legs.

Dave didn't say anything when he came to my open door for the first time in a week. He just grinned, tossed me a pair of black leather gloves, and walked away. There might have been half a second where I thought I wouldn't go, that I would stick to my guns and do what I had been telling myself I wanted. But I followed them. They knew I would. I could say I hated it, but I loved it. And I didn't really *want* to be done, when you got right down to it. It was better than drugs or booze or sex.

Once you start a thing like that, you can't just stop.

19

Pete

Lucas knew exactly where we were going. The place was only five blocks from our own. The house was nice, nicer than ours, and it pissed me off to look at it. They'd planted flowers along both sides of the walk and all their empty beer cans were on the back porch in a green Rubbermaid trashcan with a black plastic bag in it. The grass was a perfect green carpet--even the fallen leaves looked like they'd been trained to land in the neatest, most organized positions for maximum charm. There were four cars in the pristine white patch of gravel behind the house, all of them newer models and clean, with sunroofs and leather seats and deep coats of wax, garters and high school senior keys in different perky colors hanging from the rearview mirrors.

They had it all and they didn't deserve it. Their parents had been given all the easy breaks. *They* were being given all the easy breaks. Their children would have them. Their grandchildren. They would marry and breed with other privileged cockroaches to keep the bloodlines safe, insuring that we would never be without people obsessed with clothes, looks and money. Mall-shopping, *Cliff's-Notes*-reading, sports-bar-patronizing, shitty-corporate-rock-music-loving, boat-owning fucking yuppie scum, born to major in Business, rise to upper management and consume, consume, consume with their over-inflated, unearned paychecks. They were the progeny of our enemy, the trophy of our enemy, and if allowed to continue unchecked, they would *become* our enemy.

They had to die.

Standing in the shadows with Dave and Lucas, just beyond the fan of blue-white light shining from a rough wooden pole at the end of the alley, I did not feel good. My stomach was twisting and burning. The muscles in my thighs were loose and quivering. Inside the black leather gloves Lucas always provided us--where and when he got them we never knew, but there was a fresh pair for each of us every time we went out--my hands were clammy and itched at the tiny webs of skin between my fingers. A bad seam was poking the heel of my palm like a needle. I could feel my heartbeat in my throat and I was damp with sweat beneath my clothes, beginning to shiver even before I noticed it was cold enough to see every breath we took.

I did not feel good. I did not feel *right*. But I was ready to follow Lucas--shoulder to shoulder with Dave, who I had known since pee-wee soccer when we were 7 years old--and destroy any living thing that crossed my path. I was going to mutilate and kill. Every nightmare I'd woken up screaming from after watching bad slasher movies as a kid was going to come alive in my hands. Only now I was the one without a face, the one whose breath was hot and moist and reeked of death, tinged with orange Hi-C, leftover Papa John's pizza and Newport Light 100's.

Dave stood behind a dumpster and pissed in the dark, the spattering sound on weed-choked gravel louder than it really was. "Hey," he said, his voice low as he shook it off and zipped himself up. "Somebody say something poetic."

I stared at him, trying to read his face for a sign that he was serious. Lucas stared at the back of the house, watching a shadowy shape move around in the kitchen behind closed blinds. I couldn't think of a single poetic thing, not even two lines that rhymed. "He's the English major," I said.

Dave and I stared at the sides of Lucas' head and waited for anything to happen. "Come on," Dave grinned, the thick lenses in his glasses catching a glint of light for just a second. "Say something profound, I double-dog dare you."

Lucas took the last drag from his cigarette, his face a glowing orange-red circle flaring out from his mouth, and tossed the butt. I didn't think he would do it.

Just when I had given up on him he spoke.

"Here comes the one that you've been dreaming of," he said, in that low, ghastly voice that I still hear in my head. *"I'm the most exalted potentate of love."*

We went in, and Dave was laughing.

20

Pete

They had knives in that place like you wouldn't believe. There were at least four complete sets of kitchen knives on the counters and in the drawers. I've never heard of a soratory bitch who could cook anything but mac-and-cheese and frozen pizza, but every one of them has enough stuff to open a restaurant. And it's usually good stuff too, not that cheapo generic Wal-Mart shit every other college loser has to deal with. Razor-sharp blades that don't lose their edges after you cut two apples. Good solid handles, hardwood or brushed stainless steel. Top-quality merchandise, and I'd almost bet whoever bought it paid through the nose for it.

The backdoor was unlocked, as usual. The girls were hot and dressed for a night on the town when we hit, having a few drinks so their eyes would have that slightly blurry fuck-me-hard look as soon as they hit the dance floor. Those girls knew what the drill was, no doubt about it. Total surprise was no longer an option for us--we'd been on TV, in the papers, in the minds and out of the mouths of all of Friedman, probably even most of America after Brokaw did

a quick piece on the investigation on the *NBC Nightly News.*
Once they saw us standing in their house uninvited, they
were on the move and screaming. I hit the circuit box by the
basement door for good measure and killed the lights. We
could see fairly well with what came through the windows
from outside, and our eyes had experience with rapid
adjustment, so it only took a second or two for us to start
moving on them.

The first girl was a blonde with a *Friends* haircut and a
lavender form-fitting silk shirt, one of those with the sleeves
that stop at mid-forearm and the buttons that only come up
to right between their breasts so you see tit-crack. The hair
was different, but I recognized her. She'd been in my Public
Speaking class the year before--sat in the front row with her
hot brunette friend and giggled all the time, gave a speech
on her hero, Barbie, who according to her was the perfect
role model for girls because she showed them all how to
dress and accessorize.

I am not making that up.

I hoped I'd get to take a crack at her, but it didn't happen.
Barbie Girl tried to bolt past Lucas, screaming; he grabbed
her under the chin and reversed all of her momentum,
lifting her feet off the floor and slamming the back of her
skull into the wall. When he let go she slid down the wall
and left a snail-trail of blood all the way. She yelped,
twitched twice, and died with her eyes open. Blue eyes. The
left one was already starting to fill up with blood when
Lucas moved on, slamming the heel of his boot into her
sternum for whatever reason, caving her upper chest in.

A girl in Capri pants dodged me and tried to make the stairs that led up to the bedrooms; Dave grabbed her by the hair and yanked her back. A good chunk of hair and bloody scalp came off in his hand and he was cackling like a lunatic. He shoved her into the banister, hit her with a right hook that wasn't bad, and dropped her on the stairs. He slammed his knife into her stomach--blade-up, the way Lucas had shown us--put both hands around the handle and yanked it up toward her tits. I could smell Capri Girl's shit when the blade went through her intestines, the undigested puke-reeking garbage in her stomach. The stench filled the room, hit us like a wave, and Dave and I stared at each other in disgusted shock.

"That's bad," he winced. "It smells like--"

And I was flying backward, touching nothing until the side of my face connected with the end-table next to the sofa. The stupid bitch hadn't even been trying to take me out. She was so fucking clumsy and scared she ran right into me with those battering ram tits of hers, heading for the front door. She tried to jump over me and I got lucky, swung my knife and slit one of her hamstrings. She jerked her foot away too fast, lost her balance and fell into the front of the couch. I stabbed the small of her back a couple of times, clamped my hand down on the back of her neck to keep her down and stabbed her until my forearm got tired.

I thought she was dead. She had to be dead. I'd stuck the knife in her to the hilt at least 40 times. I'd done some bad, bad, organ-puncturing stuff to her; her guts must have looked like mesh inside. So when I let go of her and she rolled over, blinking at me with her mouth open and still alert, I almost pissed my pants.

"Oh God," she said. She didn't raise her voice, she didn't scream, she wasn't crying. It was shock. I realize that now. But in that moment, for the first time ever, I was terrified. Ice-ball-in-the-stomach, sweating, stuttering, pants-shitting afraid. Because she had to be dead, she *had* to. Nobody could live through that. It wasn't real. She wasn't human.

"Oh God," she said again, that Zombie Girl. Her voice was beginning to flutter and rise through the background noise--screams, pleading, Dave laughing, the noises of exertion coming from Lucas' throat as he destroyed something beautiful, the sound of something hard being slammed into something harder over and over and over again. "Oh God oh God *oh please don't kill me oh God!*"

I stood there feeling almost-drunk, frowning at her with a 25-lb. swollen face and my fingers beginning to cramp from the deathlock I still had on the knife handle. Saliva and thick black blood bubbled over Zombie Girl's pouty bottom lip and down her perfectly sculpted chin every time she moved her mouth to talk. Half the time no words came out. I raised my arm to stab her in the chest, which was stupid--after all the sticks I'd put around her spine and ribs the blade wouldn't have been worth shit, and there was no way it would have gone through her breastplate before it snapped off--but I froze up. She was reading my eyes from left to right, searching for something. And since my eyes could never be as hard as Lucas', she found it.

"I'll do anything you want just don't kill me!" she said. I

could make out most of it pretty clearly even through the whistling from her punctured lungs and the mouth and throat full of fluid. "You want money? I got money! I got some here and I can go get some more just please God don't kill me!"

I raised the knife again. That fucking cunt. Even at the end, totally fucked beyond repair, she was still trying to buy her way out of it. What kind of white-collar psychosis, ingrained from birth, does it take to make something like that happen? To make you think, in the last moments of your life, that a bunch of paper and metal tokens can make everything okay again?

I felt powerful and cold, looking at her down by my feet, begging and pleading, trying to bargain with absolutely nothing. The rush was incredible, the undeniable knowledge that I was right and true and strong. She was going to die hard, and every sensory element it could possibly provide was going to stay with me, down to the most minute detail, for the rest of my life. When I got old and my life was a completely worthless cycle of soft food and bad television I didn't understand anymore, reliving the memory of this would be my sole inspiration for continuing to draw breath, and it would be enough.

"I don't want your fucking money," I said.

Dave looked up from a throat he'd just finished hacking through, blood splattered all over his cheeks and glasses. He was making a bigger mess every time we went out, for reasons known only to him, and it was beginning to bother me. "Speak for yourself, asshole. Hey, Miss? Excuse me,

Ma'am? How much money are we talking about?"

Zombie Girl flinched as if she'd been slapped. If I was the lone monster in her world, she had a chance. You can bargain and plead with an individual. Against a team, there is no hope. This is the basis of governments, of religions, of guerilla rebels in the jungles of third world countries, of chambers of commerce and collegiate offices of admissions.

"Oh God," she sobbed. "Don't kill me you guys, I'll do anything you want... I swear to God... *oh God... oh Jesus no...*"

Dave looked at Lucas, but he wasn't smiling anymore. Zombie Girl's voice was sickening, the raw emotion in it. "What do you think? Let her go?"

Even now, I don't know why he asked. We never let anybody go, ever. It just wasn't part of the deal. Kill, overkill, and get out. No mercy, no hesitation. Dave couldn't have actually believed that she would live. I might have let her, maybe. But Lucas?

Not a fucking chance in hell.

Lucas lit a cigarette and looked at a row of decorated Greek ass-paddles on the wall, each one hanging from a thin rawhide loop knotted through a hole drilled in the handle. They were painted in pinks and greens, with butterflies and turtles and sunflowers and vines. Lucas took one down, hefted it in his open palm for weight, and stared at Zombie Girl through the tangled, sweaty curtains of his hair.

"Too religious."

He crossed the living room in five steps and grabbed a handful of her hair, jerking her butt up off the floor. He pounded her head and face with the paddle until there was nothing left of her but mangled pulp and the flat, greasy sound of someone shaping hamburger patties on a kitchen counter. Blood and fluids sprayed the couch, his clothes and the carpeting with every whack after the first dozen or so. He stopped when the paddle split through the middle and a jagged half fell onto Zombie Girl's lap.

I pressed my mouth into my shoulder, the smashed side of my face throbbing hot and dull in time with my heartbeat. It felt like my cheek was full of a thickening fluid that would find a way to leak out at any second. I was going to be sick.

"Fucking awesome!" Dave muttered to himself.

Lucas opened his mouth to say something--only the worst parts of hell may ever know what--and caught sight of his reflection in the narrow full-length mirror on the wall by the front door. He stared into his own face for a few breaths, then drew his arm back to shatter the mirror with the chunk of broken, bloody paddle still in his hand. I squinted, my eyes barely open as I took deep breaths through my mouth and tried not to vomit. With the stink of Capri Girl's opened guts still hot and heavy in the room, I was fighting a losing battle. I waited for the sound of exploding glass and swayed on my ankles. Everything was silent.

Then, from upstairs, a muted sneeze.

My eyes were wide open again. The three of us stared at each other, slow grins spreading across Dave and Lucas' faces. Lucas leapt over the back of another couch with a grace I didn't know he had in him and was gone, leaning down to yank a knife out of a dead girl's chest before he took the first three stairs in one leap and disappeared into the top of the house.

Dave backhanded me in the chest to get my attention. "Room to room," he said. "Nobody else. And don't puke, or it's that precious DNA you're so worried about."

He made a few clumsy leaps over the bodies on the floor; there were at least five that I could see. Between getting my head smashed off the table and my failed attempt at Zombie Girl, I hadn't gotten a single one of them. I had always been the number three spot on the tally sheet--Lucas on top and Dave fairly close behind, usually with assistance from one of us--but this was a new low. All my nerves and paranoia and mental-masturbation bullshit, and I hadn't done a single one of them. We never kept score officially, but everybody knew what was what. I couldn't even give myself partial credit for Zombie Girl, because she was still talking and alert when Lucas finished her off.

When we got home, this was going to be embarrassing.

I walked slowly around the room, sweating like a Russian racehorse. The place was a Jackson Pollack painting of a battlefield, every imaginable surface splattered in blackish red lines of gore. What Lucas had done to Zombie Girl at the end was almost anti-climactic when I looked at what he and Dave had done to the others. Bodies lay every which way on the carpet, at wrong angles across and against the overturned furniture. Even in the dark I could see the damage they'd inflicted was the worst I'd ever seen them do. The smell of feces and urine and hot opened guts clung inside my sinuses and mouth like fresh paint. I was going to puke, no doubt about it.

I squinted into the darkness of the kitchen and tried to make my way to it, intending to vomit in the sink so I could run some water and get rid of it with a minimum of fuss. The house was silent again. Dave and Lucas were creeping around somewhere, looking for the last one, and I had no doubt they were enjoying themselves to the fullest extent a human being can.

I was afraid.

21

Dave

I've been in so many houses, especially in the dark and uninvited, that if somebody says "Hey, remember that one?" I'm usually like "No, not really," cause they all mix together in my head. One dump is the same as another, and if it's not yours, it's a dump. The place we lived in was a craphole too, but apparently--and this is just an observation--it's possible that somehow you feel completely justified in explaining away your own piss-poor taste as a result of circumstance or kitsch even while you show no mercy in your criticism of others in this same area. Everybody's a shallow fuck, me included. The only difference is, I fully recognize that and have no problem with it whatsoever.

But anyway, yeah. So that house, it was all fancy for a bunch of 20-something jack-offs, us and the bitches included, and it was big. It had an upstairs, I know that, cause I remember following Lucas up there and looking around for him. Lucas may be the world's only 285 lb. ninja, no kidding. I knew he was up there, because there was only one set of stairs, and I'd seen him go up but not come down, and I still couldn't find him anywhere, or the chick who sneezed. I didn't look too hard. If I snuck up on Lucas' blind side in the dark like that, the only prize I'd win for finding him was a knife in the guts, which definitely would have been an anti-climactic end to what had so far been a really lovely evening. Basically I stayed near the stairs, listened for him, watched the dark for a moving shape, and when I didn't find one, went back down.

Pete was definitely *not* a ninja. I snuck up on him easy--he was stumbling around the kitchen with a knife in his hand, jerking his head around like a cat with Tourette's. I watched him look over a counter, around the side of the fridge, and sigh like wistful philosophy major contemplating the cosmic weight of her menstrual cycle. Then I jumped into the room so hard the glasses rattled in the cabinets.

"Gotcha," I said.

He brought his knife up. "You fucking asshole! I almost stabbed you."

Ooooooooh, scary. The guy I'd just seen stab a chick 943 times and not only *not* kill her, but then stand there and hold the kind of conversation you might hear if Pamela Anderson showed up on stag night at a *Star Trek* convention.

"Find anything?" I said.

"No." He was trying to catch his breath, though I'll be goddamned if I know how it got away from him in the first place. So far, he hadn't done jack squat. "Must be upstairs."

"Keep an eye out down here," I told him, just for the sake of being bossy and getting under his skin.

I headed for the stairs again, breathing through my mouth. Jesus, did we wreck that place. I bet they had to burn it to get the smells out. If they put up a memorial playground or tampon statue or whatever on the site, it will probably still reek like a dead chick's guts from March till October.

22

Dave

I saw Lucas right off the bat this time, standing in the hallway between two open bedroom doors with his head cocked slightly to the side. Somebody sneezed again and he was gone. Seriously. I blinked, and no more Lucas. I always meant to ask him if he'd teach me how he does that, but it seemed kind of gay. Dorky-gay, not butt-fucking gay. He could do it anywhere. It drove Pete completely batshit. We could be in line at the student union Burger King, people jammed in on us asshole-to-elbow, and one of us would turn around to say something to Lucas and he was gone. And it's not like he's hard to pick out of a crowd. Let's face it, the man is a behemoth.

The hallway wasn't that big, but I took my time moving up to where I'd seen him last; that whole knife in the guts thing was still in effect. When I finally saw him--standing in the middle of what looked like a laundry hamper explosion in one of the chicks' rooms--it scared the crap out of me, which was completely ridiculous. I had to put my hand over my mouth to keep from laughing.

I puckered up my lips and blew three times fast, the signal Pete had come up with after almost having his head taken off by Lucas five or six times. You didn't whistle, you just made a noise like a really timid chick in Lamaze class. It was a good plan, even if Petey the Pirate did come up with it, because if you didn't know what to listen for, it wouldn't mean anything to you and you probably wouldn't even notice it.

But anyway, I gave the signal, and Lucas waved me into the room without turning around. "Did you find her?" I whispered, so quiet that you couldn't hear much more than my mouth moving around.

Lucas nodded and pointed to the bed. I nodded and changed to an overhand grip on the butcher knife while he hooked one of his gorilla paws under a corner of the frame. We counted it off on my fingers--one, two, *three*--and Lucas yanked up. The bed flipped over and smashed a lamp on the table beside it, exposing the girl hiding underneath it, rolling around like a cockroach in old homework papers, dust bunnies, and about 15 pairs of dirty panties. She screamed and rolled over on her back. I stabbed her until she started gargling her own blood. She died. Lucas flipped the bed frame back on top of her and slapped the mattress and box springs over so they weren't just standing there like polyester-covered Stonehenge pieces. It would be a nice little surprise for the badge-sporting dickheads who cleaned up after us.

"How'd you know where she was?" I said.

"Her foot was sticking out."

I had to snort at that. "Stupid bitch. This is easier than a 14 year-old with no dad."

Lucas kicked a cluster of dirty clothes with the toe of his boot to get some of the blood off of it and yawned. "Where's Pete?"

"Downstairs on lookout."

Pete yelled. We looked at each other.

I shook my head. "So much for 'easier than…' whatever I said."

23

Dave

"Holy shit," I said, "she fucking killed Pete!"

Lucas took a step toward the bitch with the knife and she swung it in his direction to keep him back. She might as well have lifted up her shirt and flicked her titty at him. She took steps back and he took steps forward, so there was always the same distance between them. He didn't say anything and he didn't smile, just stared at her with no expression on his face and kept coming at her.

She found the phone on the kitchen wall with her empty hand and took it off the hook. When she stopped moving, he stopped too. "Okay, *okay*," she said. Her voice was shaking so bad I could barely understand her. "I'm gonna call the cops and don't you fucking move."

He took another step toward her.

"You stay the fuck away from me!" she screamed. "I'll fucking kill you!"

"I hope you know that's murder," I said. "Sugarmouth."

"Shut up!" she cried. "Everybody just shut up! I'm calling the cops, and they're gonna come get you sick fucks, and you're gonna *fry!*"

"That's it, I'm outta here," I said. I hated to miss a second of it, since she was apparently one of the rare ones who wasn't going to beg for her life. I ran out the front door and slammed it behind me, the circled around the back of the house again.

Pete had either not locked the back door behind us like he was supposed to, or he'd unlocked it again for some reason. It was probably the last thing he'd ever done right, and it was by accident. If you're looking for the meaning of his life, feel free to quote me on that.

"Yeah, see?" she was saying when I came up behind her. "Your buddy's got the right idea, you freak. If you're smart you'll go with him."

Lucas didn't move; his eyes flicked my way to let me know he'd seen me. "Get out of here!" she screamed. "Just *go!*"

He moved then, one step forward, and half of his face disappeared into the shadows again.

"I'm calling the police!" she told him.

"I don't care," he said.

"Oh God," she said. "Why? Why don't you care? Why are you doing this?"

"Because even if it means I have to *fry,*" he said, "I'm

gonna kill you, you sorority cunt."

We both jumped on her at the same time and stabbed the fuck out of her. I don't think we ever got anybody like that, before or after. I hacked her wrist to make her drop the knife and we just tore her up. By the time we let up she was more hole than skin and blood was pumping out of her in gushes and spurts.

"Goddamn it," I said, panting like a bitch. "That was close."

Lucas was breathing harder than normal, but compared to me he was taking a nap. To look at the two of us you'd think I'd be in better physical shape than that big asshole, but then again, no one's ever gonna accuse you of knowing beeswax from a blowjob, are they?

"How'd she get by you?" he said.

"Hey, I checked the closets and everything. She must have come through the kitchen." Even if it wasn't true, it sounded good. After all, it's not like Pete could throw the blame back on me unless he rose from the dead. And if he did that, I had a lot more to worry about than looking like a jackass.

Lucas pulled off one of his gloves and took a penlight out of his back pocket, which was a new one for me. He shined it around the kitchen a couple of times until we found the open basement door.

"Son of a bitch," I said. "You think there's anybody else?"

"Check it out," he said. "And turn the lights back on."

When I flipped the lever on the breaker box the whole house lit up again. Boy, did we make a fucking mess of that place. "And God said unto them 'Let there be light,'" I told Lucas. "And when He saw what He had created, He said, 'Man, does this suck.'"

Lucas was not incredibly amused by this. He put his redneck mechanic piece of crap penlight away and pulled his glove back on. "Check it over good, then wait for me here. I'll take the upstairs."

You would think that I am not one to take direction, that my inner wild-man would prevent me from doing anything that anybody tells me to. And you know what? You're right. Way to go you. Happy fucking birthday. But Lucas always seemed to know what he was doing, one way or another. Plus, if he wanted to, he could snap my neck like a fat red kindergarten pencil all pocked up with bite-marks, which is not what anyone wants to happen. Anyone meaning me, of course, because I'm an ego-maniac and deep down inside I truly believe that the whole world revolves around me. This planet is my satellite. I should charge rent, seriously. As far as money-making scams go, it would be a lot better than working at K-Mart, which I did for three weeks one time until I had a nightmare about it and quit, because who needs that crap for minimum wage?

So I checked the basement, which was pretty swank compared to the one in our dump, but nothing too special. They had a computer and a big TV and some couches and crap, probably where they did the introductions before they got right into initiating the new chicks with some aggressive lesbian and gang-bang rituals, but there wasn't really any place to hide out or anything. There was a frilly crapper and sink off to one side, and I looked around for some of those pills Lucas likes so much, but all I found was toilet paper (the aloe kind, because not even a frat rat likes to sodomize a chick with a butthole that's anything less than silky smooth) and some tampons. We could have used the toilet paper, because at our house we'd been using paper towels for like a month. And not Bounty, either--the rough brown kind you had to crinkle up a bunch of times to prevent easily-infected lacerations. But I didn't feel like carrying it around, so I left it.

Upstairs I could hear Lucas redecorating the place in his own special way. He was really going to town on it, from the number of loud crashes and shattering sounds. I didn't have to wait on him long once I got back to the kitchen. "Anything?" he said.

"Just us and the stiffs."

We ambled into the living room to take a look at Pete. He was still dead. "What do we do about this?" I said, sticking the toe of my shoe under his forehead and lifting up on it so I could see if that soratory bitch had done anything really cool to him, like gouging his eyes out. She hadn't, of course. Unoriginal bitch. One side of his face looked like somebody had shoved a golf ball under his skin, and I'd already laughed about that once, so the novelty was gone. The Stupid Bitch Award of the night went to our man Petey the Pirate his own bad self, for apparently falling on his own knife.

Lucas lit a cigarette. "Leave him."

He looked over to the right and saw a perfect footprint in

blood on the carpet. Mine, because I could see most of the word *Airwalk* in it.

"That's not good," I said. "What do we do, cut it out?"

Lucas shook his head. "Too obvious." He grabbed one of the dead chicks laying nearby and dragged her by the hair until he could rub the back of her smashed, bloody head into the footprint and mess it all up. "See any more?"

"No," I said. "Is it strange that I don't know whether to puke or just go with the fact that I might be really turned on right now?"

"Get turned on. The mess is easier to clean up."

"What about the knives?"

"Toss 'em."

So we chucked the soratory bitches' fancy-ass cutlery into different corners of the room and I turned off the living room lights again. As soon as I did I could hear sirens, because life is freaky like that sometimes. "Who picked up the Bat-Phone?" I said.

"Somebody heard the screams," Lucas said, and headed for the back door.

"Nice knowing you Pete, you dead piece of shit," I said, and slapped him on the back. "Give Satan my e-mail address."

24

Dave

Jesus Christ, did we *run*. Me, being the lazy piece of shit Generation-X product of America that I am, had shin splints and a cramp in my side the size of a frying pan after two blocks. Plus I felt like there was a very real chance I was gonna have sudden explosive diarrhea, which is never a good thing. Especially when you're running because a bunch of cop cars are hunting you like the gorillas on horseback in *Planet of the Apes* and you can't remember if you washed a bunch of chicks' blood off your face.

Pretty exciting stuff, eh?

Man, do I not like running. Some people--my mom, fucking idiots like that--say that God is fair and good. But there are people in wheelchairs, people who were born with one foot pointing toward their ass all the time and stuff like that, who stay awake at night dreaming about how great it would be to go for a run or sprint in out of the rain, and they're never gonna. It's never going to happen. That's it, they're fucked. Meanwhile, a whole legion of slackers like me--who are content to sit on the couch eating Doritos and watching *Saved By the Bell* for 9 hours straight on a perfect spring day--don't give a shit about running and never will. Between junior high school and hooking up with Lucas I think I ran twice, and both times were half-assed. There's nowhere I need to be that requires me to get there in a hurry.

Come to think of it, there's never really anywhere I need to be at all.

I kind of got off on a tangent there, but the point I originally set out to make, I think, was that God is a cuntrag. Why I felt the need to tell you this, when you either already know it or are never gonna believe it anyway, is beyond the scope of my ambition.

Anyway, so we're running through backyards, heading for home, and this huge Doberman comes out of nowhere. Seriously. Total darkness, pretty much all you can see are garbage cans and rotting picnic tables and firepits, cause we were out of the frat section and into the regular old middle-class boozer-kid part of town, and then there's this dog flying through the air with a big log chain attached to its collar like it's a kite. Lucas yanked me back just in time to save my face and dropped that dog, no kidding. One punch to the side of its pointy, toothy head and it hit the ground like Charlie Brown going for a punt, I swear to crap. The thing didn't even yelp, for chrissakes.

We vaulted over a low chainlink fence and cut across another yard. By this time I couldn't hear anything but sirens, and because most of the houses in that area are a quaint and unoriginal shade of white, everything everywhere was flashing red and blue. Total gonzo. Like one of those cheesy LSD movies from the 60's, where people wear vests and talk about peace and love and say stuff like "Groovy," and "Yeah man, this stuff is gonna blow your mind, like in a good way," and call each other "Brother" with a straight face, and make up elaborate handshakes that can only be appreciated by those under the influence of either marijuana or the cheater's high you get from dodging the draft so you don't have to go fight a bunch of peasants whose parents can't afford to unknowingly buy them some primo wacky tobacco.

I went over another fence before Lucas and stopped,

because it looked to me like we were totally screwed. The next fence we had to cross was one of those six foot wooden privacy deals, and there was no way we could climb it. I put my hands on my thighs and bent over, trying to either spit the taste of physical exertion out of my mouth or puke it up altogether. Lucas vaulted over the chainlink behind me and almost knocked me over.

"Why'd you stop?" he said. He was panting like Cujo right before he starts mauling the Pinto with the little *Who's the Boss?* kid and that chick from *The Howling* in it.

I pointed at the fence and spit again. Nasty. It came out of my mouth in a big ropy thing of drool and hung between my bottom lip and the ground.

Who says serial murder is glamorous?

"What do you want to do?" I managed to gasp out. "Turn around?"

He handed me his cigarette and I took a drag, which didn't help anything. "You gonna make it?" he said.

"I don't know," I told him. Who the hell runs and smokes at the same time? Seriously. "I think I wanna go back and take a nap with Pete."

"Come on," he said. The bastard actually *smiled* at me. What a fucking prick. "If we shag ass, we can make it home in time for *The Wonder Years.*"

He took off, straight for the wooden fence. I hung back a second so I could laugh at him when he tried to jump over it and hurt himself, but no dice. He crossed his forearms in front of his face and slammed into it, took out a whole section with a loud, rotten cracking sound and kept going. I followed him, of course. And this time I actually put some effort into it, because missing *The Wonder Years* on purpose is a disgusting display of sloth, even for me.

Some day he's gonna do something like that and fuck himself up good.

Man I hope I'm there to see it.

25

Rachel

The first thought that popped into my head when they ran past me was *You've seen him before,* but I wasn't sure where, or when. Lucas, not Dave. I didn't know their names then, though. I was standing on the deck/balcony/walkway in front of all the apartments in my building, smoking a cigarette and thinking about Punnett squares. Pathetic, I know, but I couldn't get the hang of them and the Biology test was only three weeks away. Even more pathetic when you consider that this was on a Thursday night, *the* party night when you're in college. I should have been out at the bars flirting drinks from guys and trying to find somebody to have cheap, meaningless sex with, but I'd already done that once. It only took one time for me to realize that I wasn't cut out for it.

Do you ever have those moments when you look at a random series of events and suddenly everything makes perfect sense? That's the feeling I got when they ran past. The two of them glanced up at me, just a split second of eye contact, and I knew. Granted, the sirens and flashing lights that had been flying past the apartment complex in both directions for the last ten minutes might have had something to do with it. At that point, it was almost strange to go outside at night and *not* hear sirens. They had been very busy boys.

They stopped at the dumpsters on the alley side of the complex and threw something in one of them, ducking behind it as a police cruiser swung into the parking lot. It played its spotlight along the sides of the buildings and right into my face. The cop gunned it and slammed on the brakes, stopping right below me. He threw the door open and shined his Mag-Lite in my eyes.

"You see anybody run by here?" he called up.

I told him no.

"You sure?"

"I've been out here ten minutes," I told him. "I haven't seen anybody."

"Fuck!" he barked to himself. "Go inside and lock your door."

"What's going on?" I said.

"Just do it!" he snapped. He got back in the cruiser and laid rubber. He was probably aroused. The car fishtailed around the corner of the building, past the dumpsters, and it was gone.

The two of them came out and stared at me for a couple seconds, then ran in the other direction. I took the last drag off my cigarette, flipped the butt onto the windshield of a purple Neon that belonged to one of the snotty former cheerleaders who lived in the next apartment down and went inside.

I didn't lock the door.

26

Dave

I told Lucas I thought we should kill her when we saw her, but he told me to keep running. Actually I was glad, because after all that running and crap, I was too tired to kill my grandma. Once we crossed Wheeler Street we didn't see any more coppers, and we did in fact make it home in time to catch *The Wonder Years*, although we were breathing too hard to hear most of what they were saying.

"We should get mopeds or bicycles or something," I said. "Seriously. Either that or get a harness so you can carry me piggyback."

Lucas was holding his breath for a few seconds and letting it out again in slow streams to try to get back to normal. He shook his head. "That's gay."

"I think *you're* gay," I told him. "What do you have to say about that?"

"It's possible," he shrugged.

That almost made me choke on my sugar-free Trident, original bubblegum flavor. "What?" I said.

"Never tried it," he said. "Could be getting fucked in the ass is the best thing going, for all I know."

"Wait, wait," I said. "What are you saying, exactly?"

He gave me one of those patented Lucas looks, the ones that make you feel like the dumbest piece of shit in this toilet

Earth. "You said I'm gay. I said I don't know. Never tried it. Never wanted to try it. Never will try it, most likely. So I don't know one way or another."

"Jesus Christ, that's fucked up," I said. "Let me ask you this--did you ever think about fucking a guy when you jerked off?"

"Yeah."

I had to take the gum out of my mouth and stick it on the wood paneling behind the couch before I choked on it. "Seriously?"

"Sure."

Now look, I've done that too. I read a bunch of places that all guys do at least a few times. I guess if a manly fucking man like Lucas can admit it, I can too. But just this once. And if you tell anybody, I'll track you down, cut your fucking throat, and date your corpse. Unless you're a guy, in which case I'll just cut your throat, and probably hack your wiener off and stuff it in your mouth. I realize that sounds kind of gay too, but I'll be wearing gloves and I won't get a boner while I do it, so fuck you, you hypocrite.

"You're a mess," I said. "No kidding. If I go to hell, Satan will probably make me live in your head."

"That's funny," Lucas said. He actually laughed out loud.

"What is?"

"*If.*" And then he kept laughing, the fucking asshole.

Seven and a half times out of ten, when Lucas laughs, it really makes me depressed.

27

Rachel

By the next morning I remembered where I had seen the two of them; it came to me in the shower, as I was rinsing shampoo lather from my closed eyelids. They had been in the store the day I quit/got fired. When that came back to me I could remember their faces more clearly, because I could cross-reference them-in-the-dark with them-in-the-daylight. Not well enough that I could have described them to the police, but that wasn't what I had in mind anyway.

I don't know what I had in mind, not exactly.

I really liked the murders. They were exciting. I'm basically a morbid person by nature, I suppose. Some would call that gothy, and I would shudder. I am not Goth. I don't walk around wearing a Halloween costume 365 days a year, painting my face up like a corpse and putting paper cuts on my wrists because it *lets the pain out* like those idiot girls who live in chat rooms and have online journals. I like the Cure, and Bauhaus, and Sisters of Mercy, sure. I also like the Donnas, Guns N' Roses, the early Bob Dylan stuff and everything Buddy Holly ever did. These people with their fucking labels... there should only be one label in the world. *Idiot.* Either you're an idiot or you're not. And none of this hyphenation garbage either, like they do with minorities. You're not African-American, or Asian-American, or Italian-American. You're American. That's it. So we shouldn't call them Goth-Idiots, Emo-Idiots, Punk-Idiots, Jock-Idiots, etc. They're just idiots, plain and simple.

But as I was saying, I was really into the murders. I was

saving newspaper clippings about them and tacking them to the living room wall of my apartment. And yes, I know that's lame. Not that it mattered; it wasn't like I had a lot of company. Or any company.

For me, who had read all about not only the Bundys and Gacys and Kempers, but also the really obscure serial killers that no one outside their killing grounds has ever heard of, to be in the town where a new chapter to the serial murder mythology was being born, *while* it was happening, was really thrilling. I had always wondered what it would be like to live someplace where things like that were going on, just to see what it felt like. Most of the books on serial murderers are not well-written by any stretch of the imagination, and the authors like to try to jazz it up by making it sound like a whole town is hiding under its collective bed when the sun goes down.

Something about that image that doesn't sit right and never has. Maybe 30 years ago, sure. When as a country we started to collectively realize that you didn't necessarily have to piss someone off for them to kill you, it didn't take long for the shock of it to wear off. Now, in the 21st century, there's a full-blown contingent of gorehounds and murder junkies who follow rapes, mutilations and all things macabre the way most people used to follow baseball. Death is an American pastime now. Lucas would eventually tell me why this was so, but that came later. Standing there in the shower, soaping up my unmentionables, I was still trying to figure out how I could meet him without having my soul separated from my body.

The university wasn't so big that it would take a cosmic event for me to find him. I couldn't remember seeing him on my way to or from classes, but that only meant that our schedules didn't cross paths. If you were to sit outside a building--like the University Union--for long enough, sooner or later everybody on campus would pass by. Assuming he went to class, which didn't seem like a very sure option at all.

A nest of vipers had opened in my brain, and that's a feeling I've always enjoyed more than anything else. So many possibilities, twisting and turning on each other, thoughts striking each other with razor-sharp fangs and rolling like boiling water. By the time I'd finished dressing I already knew that my classes could go fuck themselves for the day, with the exception of Biology, which had a three-absences-and-fail policy that was completely ridiculous. Not to mention unfair, since the professor had already missed seven times and turned it over to her lab assistants and other profs.

I ate a handful of Ritz and a Nutri-Grain bar, brushed my teeth and headed off with my backpack to sit outside the Union and sip Dr. Peppers until I saw a 6'3" Sasquatch with sunglasses and a black knit cap. From 8:00 to 9:45 I sat on a stone bench on the patio and didn't get anything for it but a sore, chilly behind and endless walking examples to prove the theory that intelligence is no longer a serious requirement to be accepted into college. We're talking moron central, very depressing. The internment camps the government put its own citizens of Japanese descent into during World War II have been replaced, only now we call them colleges and make parents of all ethnic backgrounds pay through the nose to send their idiot offspring instead.

I also read the school paper, but it didn't have anything really interesting about what had happened the night before, only that there was another crime scene and the police refused to comment until relatives had been contacted. I put it in my backpack anyway. There wasn't much to it, but a clipping is a clipping.

At 10:00 I had Biology lecture for 50 minutes, where we talked about how to determine a 64-square Punnett configuration for the third class in a row. None of it made any more sense when it was over then it had when I walked in, but the prof did decide to grace us with her presence. I'm sure we all made more progress because of it, and we did get to hear about the decision-making process she and her husband went through over circumcising her two sons, which had nothing to do with anything we were there for that I could see but still took up a good 20 minutes. The girl next to me complained about how hung over she was for a little while, then started talking about how she had period shits with the girl sitting next to her. Some black kid behind me with one leg of his sweatpants pulled up to the knee and his foot on the back of my seat made great contributions to the Punnett discussion, offering up a lot of *shit*'s and *man, fuck all this*'s and *when is my black ass ever gonna use some motherfuckin' bullshit like this?*'s, just loud enough to make everybody laugh and still remain anonymous.

Higher education, baby.

After class I walked down the lecture hall steps to the podium, told the prof I was having trouble getting a grasp on Punnett Squares, and asked if she could recommend a good tutor with a reasonable price. She informed me that if I would pay more attention to the lectures, it shouldn't be any problem for me to learn what I needed to know. I told her that if I paid any more attention to the lectures I would be giving them, that I had page after page of notes and was putting in a good two hours a night of bookwork trying to figure them out, and I would still like her to recommend a tutor, thank you very much. She pointed me in the direction of Fritz, the grad assistant/toady who took attendance and conducted some of the lab sections, who was beside the overhead projector flirting with two girls with oily skin, dreadlocks and hemp necklaces.

After the Grease Twins left and took most of their patchouli stink with them, I told him I needed to find a tutor. He told me that most of the tutors were all booked up for the semester, but if there were any left they would be posted on the bulletin board in the front hallway of the building--a fact that the prof apparently didn't have enough time to be aware of, what with her obsession over her sons' penises taking up so much of her thought processes. Then Fritz asked me if I had a boyfriend. I told him I was only into chicks and he told me I was cute, if I ever changed my mind to look him up at the coffeehouse he was running with his girlfriend. "It's cool," he said. "She's bi." Then he handed me a flyer for Open-Mic night and told me he hoped he'd see me there.

There were no available tutors on the tutor board charging less than $15 an hour.

I was so mad I couldn't see straight. I'd planned to go back to the Union and lurk around there for the rest of the afternoon; suddenly that didn't seem as exciting as it had in the shower, and I decided to waste the day watching cartoons and eating hot vanilla pudding with chocolate chips dropped into it, my favorite comfort food. I was starting to feel fat, but I didn't look any different, so I figured it couldn't hurt anything. I needed to start looking for another job, too. My apartment lease was paid off until January with what I'd saved working two crappy jobs over the summer, but after that it was going to be month to month, so I needed to find something that paid soon, or I was going to be playing catch-up all next semester.

I started the hike back to the apartment, my brain deep in the muck of reality. As horrible as it is to say, most of the time reality is a very depressing place to be. My head wasn't on where I was going and I missed the side path that cuts between the Earth Sciences building and the Administrative building, which meant I either had to turn around like some first-week freshman ass or keep walking and add another three blocks to the trip.

I kept walking.

A watched pot never boils, isn't that what they say? It's true, I think. My mind wasn't on anything, really--I was wondering why I had chosen to keep walking instead of turning around, even though it made the trip longer, and what my refusal to turn around and possibly look like a dufus in front of a bunch of people I didn't know, who didn't know me from a hole in the ground, meant about me as a person. Unsatisfying mental masturbation at it's finest, no real possibility for an inspirational orgasm at all. Then I looked up, and there he was, my sasquatch, crushing a cigarette out under the toe of his boot on the side stoop of the English building and walking inside.

I hot-footed it over there and looked casually through the glass double doors, but he was already out of sight. Three girls were sitting on the sides of the stoop, smoking their own cigarettes with their backpacks between their feet. I pretended to look at my watch, sat down a neutral distance away from them, and lit a cigarette of my own.

"Who is that guy?" I said. "The one who just went in. I see him all over the place."

"I think his name is Lucas something," one of them said.

"Yeah, *Lucas*," said a girl with curly red hair. She put a strange emphasis on it and grinned when she said it, but since I'd never met her, it was impossible to judge what it meant. "He was in my Shakespeare class last year." She smiled again, sort of. There was something bitter about it. "When he actually showed up, anyway."

"Yeah," said one of them. She had a red butch haircut and rings in her eyebrows. "I've had classes with him. He's almost never there, and he never says anything. *Anything*. Even if somebody asks him a question, he just looks at them and doesn't say anything. Dr. Chalmers asked us if he even knew how to talk."

The girls laughed. I did too. "What is he, like all burnt out or something?" the first one asked.

Everybody shrugged. "He's really smart," the girl with the butch haircut said. "I had poetry workshop with him, and he wrote like, the greatest stuff ever. It made some people cry--it like, *hurt* you when you read it. And in World Lit, he wrote this huge paper on *Red Azalea*, all this really heavy stuff about the emotional repercussions of communism, or something."

"That guy did?" the first girl said. "You've got to be kidding me."

"It was totally good. I worked on my paper for like, a month, and compared to his it looked like I was still in high school." The girl played with a piercing, blew out smoke, shook her head at some internal thought she didn't share.

"Maybe he's one of those really internal artistic types?" I offered. "Still waters run deep, and all that."

"Maybe he stutters really bad," the first girl said. "There was a girl in my high school like that. Every time she opened her mouth it was like Porky Pig, only 90 times worse, so she almost never said anything. She went out for the chorus, and she couldn't even sing, even though, like, you know, stuttering people are supposed to be able to sing really well. It was a total disaster. I don't think she ever got asked out."

The girl with the curly red hair smiled. "I heard him say something once."

"What?" we all said, and laughed at ourselves. The whole conversation had taken on a definite slumber party vibe.

She tucked her hair behind her ears. "I was at the liquor

store, and he was in front of me, and he had, like, four bottles of gin. The guy who works there, that cute one, with the shaved head? He said 'Can I see some ID?' and Lucas was like 'No,' and just dropped his money and walked out with the bottles."

That made all of us laugh. I didn't know any of them and didn't want to, but laughing with them felt good. I hadn't laughed with anyone else in a long time, and there is a difference.

"Gotta go," the girl with the butch haircut sighed, and dropped her butt in the small concrete cylinder full of sand beside the door. She picked up her backpack--maroon, with a tan scuffed leather bottom and two patches sewn on it, a butterfly and a rainbow--and grinned with a mouthful of teeth that weren't pretty, even though I couldn't see anything specifically wrong with them.

The others got up with sighs of their own and went in. Two of them said "bye," and smiled at me. Their teeth were very pretty, and they had good smiles. If you took a picture of them at that instant, and looked at them years later, not knowing who they were, you would still recognize that they were the smiles of people who have just shared laughter with a stranger and nothing more, innocent with a touch of interest, maybe longing. Of all the smiles in the world, those are my favorite. They make you think they could be the beginning of anything.

28

<u>Rachel</u>

I smoked another cigarette and waited out on the front stoop until my bottom started to get uncomfortably cold, then went inside. Baldwin Hall, the English and Theater building, is antique in a clean-but-crusty sort of way. There's a campus legend that the third floor, where the small one-act theaters are, is haunted. But no one's ever seen or heard anything up there except theater kids, so take that for what it's worth. Baldwin still has the original scrolled wooden doorjambs with gold leaf numbers over them, vaulted ceilings, the whole works. There are even small gargoyles on the north side of the building, although you can't really see them from the sidewalk because they're too high up. The whole place just *smells* old, like out-of-print books and floor wax and pencil shavings. It's a lousy place to have class, because the chair-desks you have to sit in are left over from the 50's or 60's, before people figured out that hard flat wood is not an ideal sitting surface for a soft round ass.

I walked every floor, peeking in all the open doors, but didn't see my Sasquatch anywhere. I lingered on the third floor, just to see if anything creepy or haunting might happen. The only thing that came close was the sound of a bunch of extroverted theater bozos pretending to be monkeys in one of the classroom studios.

I went back down to the second floor and started checking office doors, where the professors taped their schedules at eye-level, neatly typed on Xerox sheets. There were only three classes in session with their doors closed--

American Literature II, Intro to Shakespeare, and The Pedagogy of Literature. I didn't know what a pedagogy was, and since I didn't know who the guy I was looking for was either, it all clicked nicely into place and I camped out in front of that room and waited for the clock to hit 2:50 and the door to open. There was no way of knowing if my Sasquatch was in there or not. Even if he wasn't, I still knew vaguely where he would be at some future point, which was better off than I had been before.

I'd almost rather yank the hairs out of my head one by one for an hour than stand around for five minutes waiting on something to happen. Christmas morning, my period, a cop to ask for my license while I'm sitting in the car with his lights splashing off the rearview mirror and sun visors, it's all the same to me. Baldwin Hall is so old they won't hang clocks in the corridors for fear of ruining the ancient plasterwork, so I had no idea how long I'd been there or how much longer I would have to stay. By the time the ancient bell at the end of the hallway rang, I was ready to climb the walls.

Whatever a pedagogy was, it was not interesting. I've never seen so many bored, defeated faces file out of a classroom at one time in my life. The professor was still talking loudly as they left, something about a paper being due in two weeks, and she was still available for preparatory conferences, even though no one had taken her up on it yet. *Blah.* Two girls were waiting in the wings to talk to the prof as soon as she got around to shutting up, but nobody else was coming out of the room. My heart sank. I was sure I'd missed him.

And then there he was, strolling out the door with that laidback, slouching stride, as if he'd spent his whole life going from nothing important to nothing exciting. My Sasquatch. I was so excited I forgot how to talk. Strange as it sounds, I kid you not, it was just like the time I waited behind the Aragon Ballroom in the freezing cold for an hour after the Jane's Addiction show to get Perry Farrell's autograph. When Perry finally came out, looking like ten million dollars in jewels, I was completely retarded. He got on the bus, the bus pulled out, and I was standing there like an idiot with my ticket stub in my hand. I still kick myself over that every time I hear "Three Days."

And just like Perry, my Sasquatch hadn't noticed me. At least that's what I thought at the time; later I learned that he notices everything. He tucked a black and gray pen on top of his right ear, tugged the side of his black knit cap over it with two long, graceful fingers, and reached into the pouch pocket of his black hoodie for a pack of cigarettes. He had no books. I took breath when he put his hand on the double doors that opened onto the front staircase. If I'd stayed out on the side of the building, I'd have missed him.

I was close to missing him again. If he went through those doors and I said nothing, he was gone. I was sure of it. I wouldn't have the nerve to track him down again.

I took a quick look up and down the hallway. We were alone. "Run from any cops lately?" I said.

He looked at me, his hand already pushing the right side door out, and disappeared down the stairs.

29

Rachel

Lucas, my Sasquatch, paused on the front stoop to light the cigarette, his left hand up to block the wind from his lighter flame. Lit, he reached across his stomach and dropped the Bic into the left pocket of his jeans. I watched him do these things from the bottom of the wide marble stairs, inside the airlock. When he started down the eight cement steps to the sidewalk, I followed.

"I know it's you," I said. His back was to me. I tried to smile in case he turned around suddenly.

He kept walking. He had all the time in the world. I might as well have been the ghost from the third floor. There was no indication he'd even heard me.

"I saw you last night," I said, putting some pep in my step to close the distance between us. "You and your buddy. That cop asked me if I saw you, but I said no."

Nothing. Not even the slightest hitch in his stride.

"You *could* say thank you," I told him. I tried to put a snotty tone into it, hoping I could at least get a rise out of him.

He kept walking, never turned his head. We crossed the street that divides the north end of the campus from the beginning of the residential neighborhood. "I'm not gonna tell anybody, if that's what you're worried about," I said. "It's not like that. I'm not out to get you or anything."

My Sasquatch angled up a hilly stretch of grass into the

front yard of a crappy, square rent house with two huge pine trees on either side of some crooked cement steps. He climbed them, ducked under a low branch that would have scraped his hat off, and opened the powdery-looking aluminum storm door.

"I'd think you'd be a little more polite to a girl who can finger you for 57 murders," I told him from the bottom of the steps. The words were coming out of my mouth, but I didn't feel like I was in control of them. Thank God whatever *was* in charge had chosen to keep things quiet. "You guys have been so careful until now, it'd be a shame to screw all that up, wouldn't it?"

He opened the wooden door without a key and looked down at me, measuring me with his eyes. Not in a sexual way. I'm no supermodel, but my boobs are big enough that I've had enough experience with that to know what's what. My Sasquatch found what he wanted and turned into the dimness of the house, letting the storm door wheeze shut behind him. The wooden door stayed open.

I followed him and closed both doors behind me.

The house was just shy of a disaster. A maze of empty alcohol bottles and cans on every available surface, including the floor. Overflowing ashtrays. Dog-eared magazines, computer print-outs and textbooks tossed everywhere. Broken glass and pieces of at least four different telephones spread over the filthy brown carpet. The living room was a box, wood paneling on three walls and one white plaster wall that hadn't been painted or had its dents and gouges filled in years. None of the furniture matched--an ugly drab green couch, a brighter one that was made of fake bamboo with lime green leaf-print cushions, a baby blue velvety chair shaped like a horseshoe, three end-tables, two lamps that didn't have anything in common except for being big and 70's hideous, an ancient TV and VCR on one end of a cheap coffee table and a newer-looking stereo on the other.

Lucas peeled off his stocking cap and hoodie and tossed them onto the big couch, then disappeared into the kitchen. "How come you keep the blinds closed?" I called after him.

He tossed me a can of Schlitz beer and opened his own with one hand. I popped the top of my can and tried to slurp the foam that erupted from it without sounding like a pig. It was hard to make out his features in the dimness; he moved the can when he drank but not the angle of his head, and I knew he was watching me. The way my stepbrother's python used to watch the baby bunnies he threw into its reinforced plexiglass cage every six weeks or so.

"How come you keep the blinds closed?" I said again.

"Don't like to sit around with the sun in my eyes."

It was cloudy out.

I tried to make his eyes out and couldn't. My pulse was picking up. His voice was deep and he didn't open his mouth enough when he talked. The effect of this was that it took a beat longer than usual for the words to register in my head, because you had to repeat the sounds to yourself and then decipher what they meant. It resulted in a slightly nightmarish feeling, where it felt as though you were moving at a slower speed than the rest of the world and couldn't catch up.

Suddenly this was seeming like a very bad idea.

"Oh," I said. "I thought maybe--"

He raised the can to his mouth and guzzled, seemed to just open his throat and pour it down. I waited for him to crush the can and belch, but he didn't. Instead he turned back into the kitchen and disappeared. I took another sip and looked around the living room again, breathing in the stale smoke-and-beer scent of the place. As hard as I tried, I could not choke that beer down without grimacing. It was like carbonated battery acid.

Whatever I'd imagined--in the shower that morning, at least a hundred other times right after reading the articles in the paper or seeing the quick segments on the TV news--this wasn't it.

"Hey," I said after a minute or two. "Hello?" I edged toward the kitchen doorway, searching for any sign of movement. There was nothing. I put my foot across the threshold and it grabbed me, a huge fist that wrapped itself in the front of my jacket, slinging me backward into the refrigerator. Miscellaneous odds and ends on the top rattled and fell, clattering off the floor and messy countertop. Something small and hard bounced off the top of my head. My beer dropped out of my hand and hissed foam on the linoleum floor, the can rolling back and forth on its side while it gurgled out most of its contents.

My Sasquatch had a kitchen knife at my throat, the needle-tip of it poking into the tender skin just ahead of my jugular vein. It was that fast. In a blink I had gone from

Dorothy Gale, walking the fence top in a pretty little gingham dress, to a filthy bitch rolling around in mud and pig shit.

"Hey!" I cried. "I don't want any trouble! Just hear me out, okay? I don't want to get you caught, I swear."

The back door creaked open and slammed with the glass-rattling pop-and-repeat of ancient carpentry going bad. Dave dropped his portfolio case on the dirty linoleum and grinned at us. "Hey, what's this?" he said. He pushed his glasses up on the bridge of his nose with two fingers and looked at where my boobs would have been visible, if not for my jacket.

"Encyclopedia Brown here followed me home," Lucas said. His eyes never left mine, not once. Every time mine darted over to Dave and came back, he was still locked on me, waiting, an unblinking cobra. "She says she knows."

Dave took a can of Mountain Dew from the ripped case on the floor and shrugged. "That we haven't paid the phone bill in three months? That's no secret." The top of the can popped and hissed under his fingers, and he raised it to his mouth. "Ma'am?" he said. "You wouldn't happen to be that mail-order sex slave I sent away for, would you?"

"No," I said. I didn't exactly sound sure of myself.

"Six box-tops and a proof of purchase from Dirty Doug's House of Fetish? You don't know anything about that?"

I knew all the words, but nothing he'd said made any sense. The bill for my fearlessness was coming due with interest. "No," I frowned. "What?"

"That fucker!" he spat. "Three years I've been waiting for

my own slut, and he keeps saying she's in the mail. Damn it!"

I laughed without realizing I was going to and choked it off. Behind his glasses one eyebrow rose and froze above the thick black frames, as if waiting for me to tell him the punchline to a joke at his expense I'd cracked myself up in the middle of.

He took a swallow and let the hand holding the can rest in front of his stomach. "Ah, go ahead and kill her," he said.

The knifepoint stung and I saw sparks fizzling in my field of vision.

"Wait!" I shrieked.

"You mean you are the slut?"

"No," I said. "I--"

"Would you like to be?" Dave asked. "Cause, you know, I don't usually look like this. You kind of caught me on a bad day, I'm usually a lot sexier. Let me go put on my tux before you decide, okay? It'll take like two seconds."

I swallowed hard. The tip of the knife dug in when the muscles in my throat moved. "Really, I--"

"A lot of people think I look like David Duchovny," he said. "Well, not really *like* him, but kind of, you know..." He trailed off and took another drink. "Fuck it. What am I talking to you for?"

Lucas applied enough pressure on the knife to draw blood under my chin; I could feel it rolling down my skin and into the top of my shirt. "Goddamn it!" I cried. "Wait! Can't we talk about this?"

Dave smirked. "I think he just said something."

Total panic time. "It's not like that, you guys! I want to help you."

Dave angled over a few steps, probably to get a better view when Lucas cut my throat. "Why would a nice little girl like you want to do something like that?"

"Maybe I'm not so nice," I said.

Lucas tossed the knife onto the pile of dirty dishes in the kitchen sink, his eyes still locked on mine. It was no comfort. "I want to be one of you," I said, touching my wound with the tips of my fingers. In the shadows the blood was more dark than red.

Dave snorted. "Man, you don't get out much."

"I'm serious," I told him. "All those worthless pieces of shit, everybody hates them. You do something about it. You don't just sit in front of the TV and bitch--"

"Yeah, we go to church and make the honor roll and send half our money to the Peace Corps," Dave nodded. "Sally Struthers has us on speed-dial. We believe the children are our future."

"You actually go out and *do* something," I said quickly. The situation I was in wasn't hard to understand--if I let him get ahead of me or confuse me, and I lost my train of thought, I was going to die. It wouldn't mean anything to them. They might not even get around to cleaning up the mess for a few days, until the bugs got bad. The idea of my blood laying in sticky shoeprints on the filthy linoleum floor was suddenly very real and appalling. "You *do* something. You cut those fuckers down, right inside the houses their rich prick parents paid for. That's…"

My brain scrambled for the right word, the one that would keep my blood inside me where it belonged. "That's *beautiful*. That's really something. I mean, who needs another dental hygienist or her date-raping boyfriend?"

Dave laughed loudly, a high, cackling sound with a trace of a dog's surprised yap in it. It doesn't sound very appealing, I know, but it made me grin. "Where did you find this chick?" he asked Lucas.

Lucas shrugged and lit a cigarette. His eyes never left mine. He blew the first puff right in my face, naturally.

"I want to be with you," I said.

Silence. Outside the breeze was beginning to pick up, straining to become wind between the branches of trees that were already well into the nakedness of fall. Somewhere in the house I could hear wood pop as it contracted against the damp and chill.

"What do you think, Luke?" Dave said.

"No."

"So you want to get rid of her, then?" he asked. His smile was gone; he still looked oddly pleasant. "That's totally gonna fuck us on the deposit, cause there's no way we're getting that much blood out of the carpet." He held out his empty hand and Lucas handed him the cigarette, still staring at me. I tried to make eye contact with Dave. He didn't even glance at me. "It's gonna look pretty suspicious if we come strolling out of here with a bag of garbage the size of a slut."

Lucas' eyes were drilling into my brain. When he spoke, nothing moved but his lips. "So we put her in a bunch of little bags."

"I guess. But it sounds like a lot of bother, and there's still the mess to deal with."

"Let her sit a couple of hours until the blood coagulates. Wrap the pieces in dog food sacks, toss them in dumpsters all over town."

"What?" I cried. "Wait a minute, nobody's killing me! I keep telling you, I'm on your side!"

Dave's eyebrows joined in an amused frown at the bridge of his nose. "What is this 'sides' crap? Are we gonna play kickball?"

All pretensions of cool had flown out the window, leaving a trail of shit and floating feathers behind.

"What's it gonna take for me to prove it to you?" I said. I sounded desperate.

"Kill a cop."

Dave and I stared at Lucas. Dave blew out a gusty puff and grinned. "Clever!"

"What?" I said.

"That a problem?" Dave asked.

"Why do I have to kill a cop? You guys do sorority bimbos and their moron boyfriends. You never killed any cops."

"It's all part of our new 'Horrify America' plan," Dave grinned. "You want to be our first new member, you gotta help broaden our horizons."

Two things became crystal clear to me right then and there. The first was that if I didn't kill a cop, they were going to kill me. In theory I had no problem with this, because a cop is a cop is a cop, and they're all bullying assholes who aren't worth the oxygen they use. The second thing was that Dave is completely and totally full of shit, but very, very sharp. Definitely not somebody to be underestimated.

"What's next?" I asked. "Old people and little kids?"

"They're horrified enough already."

We looked at Lucas and waited for him to speak. He didn't. "When do I have to do it?" I asked.

"Tonight."

I gave him a smile, one of my best ones, in the hopes that it would be infectious. It was not. "That's kind of short notice, isn't it?" I said.

"What do you have to do that's so fucking important?" Dave snorted. "The Girl Scouts having another cookie drive?"

"You want me to go out, right now, and kill a cop?" I said, more to myself than either of them.

"Or we cut your throat and let you bleed to death over the toilet," Dave offered. "Have you seen our bathroom? Cockroaches are afraid to die in there."

Lucas lit another cigarette. I plucked it out of his mouth and took a drag and blew it out at both of them. I was feeling very, very cocky, at least on the outside. "I never liked cops anyway," I said.

Dave waited until I put the cigarette between my lips again and then snatched it, shaking his head at the lipstick on the butt before putting it in his own mouth. "You might be surprised. People's personalities change a lot when they're dying on your shoes."

"Impending doom will make a cop likable?" I frowned.

"Hey, if you want to work miracles, go bother Jesus and drink his fucking beer," Dave told me. "All we do is kill assholes."

30

<u>Dave</u>

I wouldn't say I liked that chick right off the bat, exactly, but she had definite potential. The fact that she was a chick was going to be a pain in the ass, but she smelled good and seemed like she might have at least three-quarters of a brain in her head. She barged into the Splat Cave and didn't get all pissy, even when Luke gave her throat a little love-cut, so that was something. Plus, at that point, I would have been ready to offer that fucking frat pussy with the broken arm a beer and let him watch *Dawson's Creek* with me, just for some conversation. Don't get me wrong--I like Lucas. He's a riot, when he actually says something, which is about as often as the women's Olympic gymnastics team stocks up on tampons.

After we got done with our little *Reservoir Dogs* standoff in the kitchen, we watched a lot of TV. Lucas and I drank some beers, I ate most of a 5 lb. brick of Rice Krispy Treats that Pete had been hiding under his bed, and that Rachel chick and I made some good jokes. Nothing very exciting. When *The Wonder Years* was over, Lucas got up and went out to the car, and we followed him.

We drove to the Wal-Mart parking lot and sat on the hood

of the car smoking cigarettes for a long time. It was after 10:00, the place was closed, nobody there, no other cars except for a rusty gold mini-van that had been sitting there for like three weeks straight. That chick was trying to play it cool, but she was twitchy.

"We've been here a half hour already," she said. "What the hell are we doing?"

Lucas spit. Now I'm not above spitting if there's something bad in my mouth, but he does it for no reason at all, like all the time. At first I thought it was kind of gross, because it is, but then I guess I just quit thinking about it.

"It's called being patient," he said.

"Cops always patrol the lot about now," I told her. "You gotta keep the world safe for democracy."

She rolled her eyes. "By guarding toilet paper that sells for 25% less than its competitors?"

"Hey," I said, "cheap toilet paper is what separates us from the Russians. Did you ever see a democracy run by people with raw, dirty asses? That's what I thought."

"Well if cops protect toilet paper as well as they do sorority girls, we're gonna be here awhile before any show up," she said, which I thought was pretty funny.

The cop car showed up like two seconds later, I swear to crap. It came down the main drag and turned into the parking lot to do its usual check for rednecks trying to steal motor oil or fishing lures or whatever, and slowed down when it saw us sitting there like the slack-jawed losers we are. Lucas did that freaky trick with his head where he turns it to the side and flexes his neck and something pops really loud, then stood up and flipped his cigarette butt. "Hit me," he said.

This was too good. I had no idea what he was up to, but who am I to turn down an opportunity to try and make hamburger out of that big asshole's ugly face? "No punch-backs," I said, and that chick giggled way more than was necessary.

Lucas gave me one of those one-sided grins and raised an eyebrow. "Come on sweetie, while we're young. And try not to chip a nail."

I drew back, total old-school WWF style, and slammed my fist into his cheek. He threw himself backwards across the hood and knocked that chick off onto the ground. I shook my hand to get some of the pain out of it. I thought I broke knuckles for a minute there, maybe even my whole hand and wrist, no kidding. I was gonna be jerking off with my blind-date hand for at least a week.

The cop hit his cherries and the gas and came flying up on us; Lucas shoved me back against the car. It was a good shove, but he was taking it easy on me. Good thing, too. That goon could probably rip my kidneys out and make me piss in my own face if he wanted to.

The chick picked herself up and said "Jesus!" or something like that, but she figured out what was going on in like two seconds and started waving her arms at the cop and screaming for help. He stopped about 20 feet away from our car and jumped out with his hand on his gun, and that chick ran over to him and latched onto his arm.

For a second there, I realized just how totally fucked we

would have been if she'd been lying to us, or changed her mind about all that crap she'd said back at the house. All she had to do was yell *It's them, they're the killers, save me!* or something to that effect, and Lucas and I would have probably each gotten three warning shots in the back.

"You have to stop them!" she screamed. "They're killing each other!"

The cop jerked his arm away from her and held her off. "What's going on here?" he oinked.

Since things were going the way Lucas wanted them to-- or at least I guessed they were, since he never actually *bothered to fucking tell us* how they were supposed to go-- I figured we were back on some terra firma. Luke and I were wrestling each other around, making it look good for the cop. When I saw Luke glance over toward that chick, I nailed him one right in the lip. Seriously, when was I ever gonna get a chance like that again? Fucking never, that's when.

Lucas tasted his bottom lip with the tip of his tongue to check for blood and grinned at me. There wasn't any blood. I grinned back at him, because I'm charming like that. He was so gonna kick the shit out of me when we got home.

"This fucking piece of shit, all I wanted was a fucking ride out here to get some Blistex and the place was closed, right?" I told the cop. Really loud and obnoxious-like. All those times Lucas made us watch *COPS* was finally coming in good for something, at least. "So I go up to the doors to see if somebody will let me in, and when I get back he's got his goddamn meat hooks all over her. I'm a *man*, goddamn it. You ain't gonna fuckin' disrespect *me* like that and just walk away. I'll *kill* you."

I looked at Lucas, yelled "I'm gonna fuckin' *kill you!*" and jumped in his direction. He grabbed me by the front of the shirt, threw me across the hood, and came after me with one of those awesome *Dukes of Hazzard* hip-slides I sprained my ankle trying to do once when I was like nine. When he had me down on the ground, that fucker put his knee right into my nose. Not hard enough to break it, just enough to make it bleed, set off fireworks in my skull, and make my mouth taste like dusty jeans. Not pleasant, but I guess I kind of had it coming for socking him one in the mouth when he wasn't looking. And I wasn't going to have to worry about him tying me into a pretzel when we got home, so that was something.

The cop grabbed both of us by the collar and pulled us apart like little kids, which cracked me up. "Cut the shit!" he screamed. "I want to know which one of you animals threw the first punch, and I want to know right now!"

Behind him I saw that chick lift up her shirt and pull the knife Lucas had given her out of the sheath she'd tucked into her pants. It was a big knife; I was hoping she'd have to pull the shirt up high enough that I could see her tits, but no dice.

"What fucking difference does that make?" I spat. "What, you're gonna throw my ass in jail and let this piece of shit go home and fuck my girl? Is that your idea of justice, you fucking pig?"

You know what? There's not too many things in life that

make you feel more manly than talking shit to a cop and getting away with it. Well, kind of getting away with it. I could have done without the part where he let go of Lucas, threw me on the ground and started choking me with his nightstick, but nothing's perfect. Except me, of course.

"What did you just call me?" the cop yelled in my ear. Talk about some rank breath. I think he must have spiked his coffee with rotting brownies. "I don't care *who* threw the first one, scumbag. Your ass is going to jail. And I hope your buddy fucks her in the *ass* for you. *Twice.*"

He stuck his knee on the back of my neck and put me in one of those thumb-locks so he could get the cuffs on me, which is when that chick finally decided to stop powdering her puss and hack his throat with the knife. He turned around to fight her off and she stabbed him in the cheek. He fell over groaning.

I rolled away and stood up, rubbing the back of my neck. "What were you waiting for, Christmas? He could have choked me to death," I said. The front of my t-shirt was totally soaked with blood. I think most of it was mine. "Shit," I said. "You think I'm gonna have to wash this before I can wear it again?"

The cop was trying to crawl over to his car on his belly, but he was slow. You would be too, if most of your bodily fluids were spraying out of your neck. Lucas took a two-step start and punted his face for a field goal with one of those shit-kicking steel-toed motorcycle boots he wears. The cop's nose fucking *exploded.* No kidding. Some of his teeth even fell out, I think. His forehead hit the pavement and he

166

started crying like a little bitch.

"Don't do this oh God don't do this," he said, really boo-hooing it up. "I got a wife and daughter, I'm begging you--"

"Finish him off and let's go," I said. "I'm hungry."

That chick was shivering like an epileptic Chihuahua, but she looked pretty happy. She kept looking back and forth between Lucas and me, waiting for one of us to tell her what she should do. Fucking amateur. Finally she grabbed the cop by the hair, pulled his head back, and sliced him from ear to ear. When he went from sobbing to gurgling, it wasn't hard to see he didn't have much time left.

"I hope somebody fucks your *daughter* in the ass, you pig piece of shit," she said, and drove that knife right into his ass. Not the cheek, either. In the middle.

"Man," I said. "Not a big fan of anal sex, I take it?"

"My stepdad was a cop."

"Not a big fan of assholes in general, then," I said.

She nudged him with her toe. "Is he dead?"

"I don't know, ask him."

"Shut up!" she said. "How am I supposed to know? I'm not a doctor." For a second there I thought she was going to cry, which would have been bad. I don't really do the whole comforting thing. And compared to Lucas, I'm like a white male Oprah.

"Maybe not a regular doctor, but I'd say you have definite potential as a proctologist," I told her, and lit the cigarette Lucas handed me. "Let's go, before McDonald's closes."

"You're gonna go in dressed like *that?*" she said.

Chicks. Can't live with 'em, can't hide their bodies in

water because their tits float, I always say. "I just put these pants on last week," I told her. "Besides, why do you think they invented drive-thru?"

She made one of those snotty chick faces and looked at the huge pool of blood around the cop's head. "He was right, you guys are animals."

"This coming from a chick who just shoved a knife up a guy's ass," I reminded her.

"He was asking for it."

Lucas took the knife out of the cop's butthole, wiped the blade off on the back of his uniform pants, and put it back in the holster. We got in the car.

"You know what would really kick ass?" I said. "Serial killer Happy Meals. A free ski mask and nylon rope in every box."

"What would the girls get?" Rachel said.

"They don't get shit. Chicks don't appreciate good toys."

We went out the back side of the parking lot and Lucas left the headlights off for a few blocks, until we were sure there were no other cars around. I waited for that chick to come back at me with something, but I think I stumped her on that one.

31

Rachel

My body was a bundle of nerves as I sat in the cramped backseat of Lucas' hot rod Camaro, the kind of car I had always promised myself I'd never ride in even if I was stranded beside the highway in a blizzard and it was the only car I'd seen for hours. I *knew* we were going to get caught. I knew it like I know that I'm right-handed and that I hate corn, no matter what form it comes in or how it's prepared.

The notion that the police might swoop down on us from anywhere at any time and take us into custody was a rush full of a giddy, rotting kind of sickness. Every alley had a cop car in it at first glance; every intersection was a possible trap. They were going to get us, and we deserved it. *I* deserved it. I had killed a police officer, theoretically the worst crime you can commit in any nation in the civilized world.

Theoretically. Because let's face it... who in their right mind wouldn't want to kill a cop?

All my life I had heard the phrase *in cold blood*. When you murdered a person for no apparent reason, that's how they described it. *In cold blood.* Imagine my surprise as I realized that the only cold blood in our situation belonged to the cop, and was probably already beginning to thicken and gel on the gritty blacktop of the Wal-Mart parking lot. I was so hot I almost couldn't stand it; my face felt like that boiler in *The Shining* right before it blows everything to kingdom come.

But I felt good.

I felt *alive.*

I also had the same sensation I'd had right after losing my virginity--that inadequate nakedness, overwhelmed by the sudden realization that I had absolutely no idea, once the act was over, what I was supposed to do next. And, if you want to pervert the analogy further, Dave and Lucas were not the most helpful or understanding of lovers. Dave, who never seemed to be at a loss for something to say, was rattling off a long and detailed argument about why he believed Jerry Springer was a better role model for young girls than Oprah Winfrey--some of which made sense, in its own peculiar way, and none of which I can remember now. I suppose calling it an argument wouldn't be right, exactly, since Lucas was listening but not saying anything. I tried to think of a way to come up with two cents of my own to throw in, but my brain was flying around inside my head in a million jagged fragments.

"Goddamn it!" Dave yelled. I had to blink myself together before I realized he was looking back at me. "Why do you keep kicking my seat?"

I stared at him, numb and dull. "What?"

"Why the hell are you kicking me?"

"I'm not," I said, looking down at my bouncing knees for the first time. "Am I?"

"Why would I make something like that up?"

"I don't know," I offered weakly, and giggled. "Why would you?"

"I don't mind if you feel the urge to be irritating," he said. "Personally, I'm a fan of irritation in all forms that don't involve my skin or genitals. I *live* for irritation. But at least try to be clever about it, huh? I mean, really. Come on, kid. Get with the fucking program."

He turned back to Lucas. "Where was I?"

Lucas eased to a stop just before the oil-spotted concrete

pad in front of the McDonalds drive-thru sign. "You were about to give me the money to pay for the food you're gonna order."

"No I wasn't."

Lucas looked at him. "Yes you were."

"Are you sure?"

Lucas stared.

"Okay, okay," Dave said, and leaned over on one hip to dig the money out of his pocket. His hands were awkward on the bill, almost like he was afraid it would disintegrate if he handled it too roughly. "I've got five bucks. What's the most I can get for that?"

Nobody answered him. I was locked into what was apparently my own one-girl trip through the hell of paranoia, and Lucas--well, Lucas is just Lucas. I wasn't exactly sure what that meant yet, but I had the feeling I was almost through the prologue and ready to begin chapter one of that particular book.

Why the fuck are we stopping at McDonalds and arguing over Chicken McNuggets when we just killed somebody? I wanted to scream at the top of my lungs. Too, too surreal. The smell and taste of that cop's blood were still in my nose, on the back of my tongue, inside the fillings in my teeth, and I couldn't get rid of it. For all I knew, sitting in the darkness of Lucas' back seat, I had it all over me. Had I looked myself over before I got in the car? I couldn't remember. I thought I had. I knew I didn't. The world was rushing warp-speed around the car and inside of it we were on our own time, moving with the most maddening slowness I had ever known. We were ripe to be overtaken, and we would be. I knew it.

We got Dave's food. We went to the liquor store; Dave and I stayed in the car in silence while Lucas disappeared inside and returned with a case of Keystone Ice and a brown paper sack that clinked with bottles. We went back to their house. They turned on the TV just as *The Wonder Years* came on again. Lucas handed out beers, lit a cigarette, sat in the baby blue velvety horseshoe chair. Dave ate. And ate. And ate some more.

It was revolting, the way he ate without even seeming to notice the blood that was drying all over the front of his t-shirt and khakis, but after the second beer my brain just sort of turned its back on the whole subject. If I didn't look at it, it wasn't there. Simple as that.

Eventually he looked into the paper sack between his feet and groaned. "You know what's wrong with this country?" he said. "If you go someplace and say 'Hey, give me four cheeseburgers and some fries,' and then you go home and eat all that stuff, there's never anything else in the bag. You'd think they'd just say 'Hey, this guy sounds hungry, and we're just going to cook all this crap sooner or later anyway, so let's give him a couple extra burgers.' I mean, that seems fair to me."

"How could you eat all that garbage and still be hungry?" I said.

"Don't change the subject. We're talking about the greed of the capitalist society we live in."

I held my hand out and Lucas put another can of beer into

it. "So you're saying the main problem with America is that the inherent greed of a capitalist society somehow manages, by its very existence, to drown out the pathetic bleating of your own gluttony?"

Dave's eyes were shining. I had piqued his interest. "Yes."

"So the entire fast food industry should only hire mind-readers."

"Exactly."

He was baiting me, and I knew it, but I didn't care. The beer had oiled up my brain and tongue, and I like a pointless argument as much as the next college kid. "That would mean that only a specific group of people could work those jobs, which means that they would have to be paid more for their services, which would raise the price of hamburgers, which means that an obviously unemployed person like yourself wouldn't be able to afford four hamburgers in the first place," I said.

He considered this, smiling. "No, but I could afford one. If I order one, they can read my mind, realize I really want nine, and just spot me the other eight."

"So we're cutting the staff down to people who can read minds," I said, "and who are also generous to the point of idiocy. Don't ask for much, do you?"

"Hey," he said. "I don't want to save the world, I just want another fucking hamburger."

There was nothing I could say to that. Not without a few minutes to sober up. I'm a lightweight drinker, without question. And by the time those few precious minutes had passed, there wouldn't be any point in saying anything more on the subject anyway. Life is a conversation. You miss your opening and it's gone forever.

"Whatever," I said instead. "So what's the verdict? Am I in, or what?"

"Not so fast there, Miss," Dave said. He was examining the stray grains of salt on the sides of his fingers as if he meant to lick them but couldn't quite decide. "You still have to compete in the cooking, dishwashing, and blowjob competitions before all the votes can be tallied."

"If you make one more reference to the fact that I'm a girl," I told him, "I'm gonna stick your head up your ass and roll you down a long flight of stairs."

"You've really got a fetish for sticking stuff up guys' asses, don't you?" he frowned. "What is that, some kind of estrogen thing?"

Lucas was staring at the ceiling, his head tilted back at a comfortable angle, his hair draped over the back of the baby blue velvet horseshoe chair and reaching halfway to the floor. There was a frosted bottle of cheap gin in his right hand; in his left he rolled three pills, three different colors, with a casual grace that was both fascinating and alarming. "How'd you like to be a duo?" I asked him.

He said nothing. Dave laughed loudly at some private joke.

"I gotta go," I said. "I've got a psych test tomorrow."

"Psych, huh?" Dave replied, on auto-pilot. He was staring at the television, wiping his fingers on his blood-stained khakis. "Maybe you can figure out what's wrong with you."

I put my coat on and opened the front door.

"Come over tomorrow, if you want," he said, still honed in on the television screen. *Taxi* was playing behind a rolling veil of lime green static. The set was a Zenith, pre-remote control, so old that it only came in clearly when it felt like it.

"See you guys," I said.

Lucas's left hand kept moving, the rest of his body still except for the almost imperceptible rise and fall of his lungs inside his chest.

Dave turned his jaw in my direction and left his eyes on the TV set. "Pleasant dreams, you murdering cunt."

32

Rachel

FRATERNITY + COMMUNITY = UNITY.

I was coming out of the student union bookstore with the latest issue of *Spin* and a badly-used copy of *The Grapes of Wrath* when I saw the sign taped up on the wall next to the Burger King. It stopped me in my tracks, literally.

Think about it.

FRATERNITY + COMMUNITY = UNITY.

Somebody had not only thought that this was clever and meaningful, but *inspirational.*

If you look at it as an algebraic equation:

$$FRATERNITY = F$$
$$COMMUNITY = CU$$
$$F + CU = U$$

Can you see the problem here? Mathematically,

"fraternity" would be a negative integer, meaning that "fraternity" takes away from "community."

You don't even need math to see a thing like that, actually. Just look around you.

The way my copy of *The Grapes of Wrath* looked made you want to take a quick peek over both shoulders to make sure you were alone, then hold it up to your face and sniff for the faintest whiff of dog urine. The front cover had been creased in so many directions it refused to lay flat, and there was an ugly brown stain running along the tops of last 200 pages or so. The laminate that was supposed to protect the surface of the book was peeling up from the corners and some idiot or idiots had written things like *ß important!!* and *Why don't they just get **jobs?*** in the margins. And, just in case there were any doubts in my mind on the subject, the bookstore had taken it upon themselves to place a thick yellow sticker with the word **USED** in black letters on the bottom inch of the spine.

Thank you, University Bookstore staff. My undying appreciation for your tireless work in overcharging me at every turn for the vital service of pointing out the obvious.

They wanted $15.95 for a new paperback copy, and $2.75 for the one in my hand. I didn't have the money for the new one. Even if I had, I wouldn't have gotten it. For one thing, that's highway robbery. For another, anybody who would pay that much for that particular book, new, wouldn't have chance one of ever understanding what it's about.

I was ready to put my headphones on and head over to Dave and Lucas' place when some bimbo stuck her pen in my face and said, oh-so-cheerfully, "Would you like to sign our petition?"

Capri pants. Sitcom haircut. Blue contact lenses that made her eyes look like badly mixed paint. Bouncy, perky tits inside a Wonderbra you could see through her white blouse. Perfect skin, teeth polished to a high gleam. She was wearing a sticker over her left boob that read **HELLO MY NAME IS HEATHER** and she was blinking three times a second. Trying to keep her eyes from turning to dust in spite of the white-hot, pointless cheer welling up inside her.

"Petition for what?" I said.

"We're trying to get the city council to put up some more rape beacons, like the ones in south quad?" she said. "Only like, in the *town.*"

"In the neighborhoods where *students* live," said one of the girls at the table behind her--**HELLO MY NAME IS LAURA.**

HELLO MY NAME IS HEATHER was nodding, nodding, nodding. "Yeah, that's what I *meant* to say."

Absolute brilliance. Blue-light special rape beacons, every few blocks, all over town. People had been pulling false alarms on the things since their installation a year before I started as a freshman, but since Lucas and Dave had decided to become an anonymous two-man force of nature, the number of falsies had skyrocketed. Our beloved school paper, *The Courier*, didn't even bother to write them up anymore, or so I'd heard.

Most of what you hear is right, one way or another.

So, worst-case scenario, if these stupid bitches got enough

names on their petition to take it to the Friedman city council, they'd be shot down for lack of funds and all their hard work would be for absolutely nothing--basically meaning that they wouldn't have anything to show for it in the way of resume-building extra-curricular activities. This was a concept I enjoyed immensely.

Best case-scenario, they could actually get the thing passed. In which case there would be more false alarms all over town, which meant that the already pathetic and ineffectual police department would be spread even thinner answering them. Not to mention the budget money that would need to be diverted for their construction, or the mess it would cause by closing streets to traffic, including cop cars.

You would have to be a complete moron to come up with a plan like that. On the surface it looked good, which is really all that counted, because shallow bitches like the ones in front of me never look past the surface of anything anyway. The whole thing was a tropical outdoor wedding in monsoon season.

"I'll sign it," I said.

"Cool!" **MY NAME IS HEATHER** said. "Thanks a lot!" She looked me over while I took her pen and wrote *Maya Ford* on the first available line. "Hey, you live in our apartment complex, don't you?"

I looked at her again. She did live next to me, four apartments down. Once when I'd set some groceries down to unlock the front door she'd staggered past and stepped on a new loaf of bread, much to the delight of her friends. I believe the slurred apology she offered had gone something along the lines of "Whatever *bitch,* like you really need to be eating *bread.*"

"I think so," I smiled, and tucked a lock of hair behind my ear awkwardly. Charmingly.

"Yeah, we're *totally* doing this as a community service project for our *sorority,*" she said.

"Yeah, not because we're like, *feminists* or anything," another girl at the table told me--**HELLO MY NAME IS DAWN.** "It's for the *sorority.*"

"You guys are Pies, right?" I said.

HELLO MY NAME IS TERI. "Yeah, all four of us!"

"Good luck with your project," I told them.

"You should rush with us!" **HELLO MY NAME IS HEATHER** said. "Everybody's really great, you'd have an *awesome* time."

I stepped closer to the table, into the hub of their activity and out of the way of people who were more than happy to try and walk through me like I wasn't even there. "Do they really make you do all that bad stuff to initiate you? Hazing and all that?"

"Oh no! It's really cool. You do some crazy stuff, but it's nothing *bad.* It's like, *zany,* or something."

"I had a friend who was a Zeta at another school, and she said they were a bunch of freaks," I lied. "So--"

HELLO MY NAME IS DAWN. "Zetas are a bunch of fucking *bitches,*" she said, glancing around to make sure no Zetas were within earshot, I assume. "You don't want to rush *them.* They *would* make you do bad stuff. They're a bunch of *sluts."*

"Oh."

HELLO MY NAME IS LAURA. "No, it's really cool over at our house. Everybody's really nice, it's like we're sisters and it's a big family. Only we all get along and everything."

"Wow, that's really great," I nodded. "I had class last semester with some Pies."

HELLO MY NAME IS TERI. "Cool! Which ones?"

Oh, what a tangled web. "Uh... Jen and Sarah," I said. "I don't remember their last names."

HELLO MY NAME IS HEATHER. "You mean Tara?"

"Yeah, that's right I think."

HELLO MY NAME IS HEATHER. "That is *so* awesome! Tara's like, one of my six best friends! You *so* have to rush with us, you already know people and *everything!* We can help you with your makeup and make you *really* cute and stuff, and show you what kind of clothes to get? You'd have *such* a great time!"

"I'm excited," I said. My voice was as flat as their asses, as their brainwaves. They didn't catch it.

HELLO MY NAME IS DAWN. "Wait, aren't you friends with that big *creepy* guy? The one who was in my *English* class? I think I saw you walking with him yesterday."

"Oh," I said, and rolled my eyes. "Him. He's just helping me with my term paper."

HELLO MY NAME IS DAWN. "That guy is a *freak.* He only came to class on test day, and I *swear* he's on *drugs.* He never said anything, *ever.* The professor was *soooo* pissed at him. He didn't buy *any* of the books and he got an *A* on every test. It was *insane."*

HELLO MY NAME IS LAURA. *"That* guy? You're friends with *him?"*

"Not really. He's just helping me with my term paper," I said, as if I had not just said the exact same thing less than 90 seconds before. "So do you think you'll get these beacons?"

HELLO MY NAME IS DAWN. "No."

HELLO MY NAME IS HEATHER. "Yeah, since that serial killer psycho got killed, they'll probably just say we don't need them anymore."

My head felt the way it does when you get off the couch too quickly. "What are you talking about?"

HELLO MY NAME IS DAWN. "Didn't you *hear?* It's in the paper."

I said something to them, I don't know what. *Late for class, see you around, I'll think about rushing, die you fucking cheerleader gangbang anal whores.* Something. I stopped at the bin by the foot of the stairs that led up to the street and fished out a copy of *The Courier.* I felt like I was going to vomit. The headline was huge and black, the kind they use for things like WAR! or *U.S DROPS THE BOMB.*

Two lines.

CAMPUS KILLER FOUND SLAIN;
FINAL TALLY 62

33

Rachel

I was a mess, total disaster in blue canvas high-top All-Stars. Should I run? Would that draw attention to me? Did it matter, now that they were dead? Where the hell was I supposed to run to, anyway?

Under the circumstances as I knew them, I did the stupidest thing possible. I went straight to the house.

I slipped up the alley, around the garage they weren't allowed to use, across the shaggy backyard in broad daylight. Like an Apache Indian in a bad, bad western--one of those guys with a lot of skin bronzer and a coarse black wig, trying to make his blue eyes hard as flint and the muscles of his face slack. That was me.

The back door was unlocked. That surprised me at first, although when you think about it, what did they have to be afraid of? If the devil locks the gates of hell, it's only to keep people from getting *out*.

That horrible tan linoleum creaked under my feet; I could hear it over the sound of Sonic Youth playing at a comfortable volume on the stereo in the living room. I had the album but couldn't remember the name. I peeked around the corner, into the living room.

Lucas and Dave stared back at me.

Breathing. Smoking. Blinking. Drinking beer.

Alive.

"Well, if it isn't what's-her-snatch," Dave said.

These were the assholes I'd been terrified that someone had killed. To be honest, because I hadn't actually taken the time to read the paper yet, I was a little insulted at the idea that they had waited until I'd gone home and then went out again without me.

There is truly no logic in the human brain whatsoever.

"You guys aren't in trouble?" I said.

Dave shrugged. "No more than usual."

"I thought you guys got busted. There's a big write-up in the paper about how they caught some guy." I flopped down on the big ugly green couch next to Dave and started digging through my backpack to show them.

Dave snorted. "Police work in the 21st century--a possible culprit falls down dead at the crime scene, then the cops show up and say 'Okay, we got him. Now give us a raise.' Fucking idiots."

I found the paper and offered it to them. Neither of them took it, and I started to scan it myself. "So then who is this Peter Bilotti guy?"

"This asshole who used to live with us," Dave said. "Do you have any gum? Like Trident, or Juicy Fruit maybe?"

"You mean he got killed and you guys just left him there?"

"I wanted to carry him home and flush him like a goldfish," Dave said, "but Lucas wouldn't let me."

I slouched down and dropped the newspaper into the mess on the floor. The wind was out of my sails. "It's nice to know what kind of crowd I'm running with," I said.

Dave held his bottle of Killian's Red up to his nose and smelled it. "Yeah. And all this time you thought we were Webelos working on some really bizarre merit badge."

"So if I get killed you guys are just gonna leave me where I lay?"

Lucas lit a cigarette. "Dave will probably fuck you before we go, if that's any consolation."

"It isn't. You think they're gonna find out it was you guys now?"

"Not unless Dave chokes on a hamburger and dies in the middle of a pile of naked girls with a knife in his hand," Lucas said. I think it was the most I'd ever heard him say.

"Officially," Dave said, making quote-fingers, "Pete lived in the dorms."

"So what happened?"

"He wasn't very good. Actually, he was kind of a bitch."

One of Lucas' eyebrows went up. "Kind of?"

"Well, he did have his good points," Dave replied. "Sometimes he'd buy me hamburgers. But then he'd make me suck him off."

"He made you give him head for hamburgers?" I said. The whole idea of it was revolting. I'm not homophobic, but the idea of going down on a guy for a greasy, nasty hamburger was really stomach-churning. Not to mention the whole issue of Dave's hygiene and anything sexual. Even if he didn't smell bad, he still looked like a walking oil slick.

"No," Dave said.

"You're a pervert."

He looked at Lucas. "Have you noticed that people are more offended by a guy sucking dick than banging corpses? You gotta have a theory or two on that."

Lucas put the ball of his thumb under the edge of a bottle cap and shot it across the room. Steam wafted out of the bottle's top, but no foam. "People hate parades."

We stared at him. "What?"

"Every year they have gay pride parades and block up traffic for hours," he said.

"And there's Broadway," Dave nodded. "And sitcoms. And the hair care industry."

"Straight people like that stuff. Nobody likes a traffic jam."

"Do you really believe that?" I asked.

"It's a theory. I don't have to believe it."

"They should have a necrophilia parade," Dave said. "Think of the floats! I'd pay money to see that." And then he just kind of left us, his brain imagining God knows what.

"Not to change this endlessly fascinating subject," I said, "but I'd really like to wipe these girls in my apartment complex off the face of the earth."

"Do it," Lucas told me.

"Yeah, really," Dave said, back with the living again. "Do it yourself."

"Wait a minute," I protested. "I'm the new kid, remember?"

"It isn't brain surgery," Dave told me. "At least not with anesthetic. And losing the patient is kind of the point."

"I don't know…" I began, and didn't really know where to go with it.

"You think we went to Psycho School on weekends? It's on-the-job training."

"I've seen slackers before, but you guys are in a class by yourselves," I said.

Both of them held up a middle finger without looking at each other or away from the television, which was on and muted. "I don't suppose you could come up with a game plan for me during a commercial?" I asked. "Something to help a beginner out?"

Dave glanced at me and back to the TV. "Lucas will."

"Why not you?"

He leaned forward to check out the action on *Thundercats* snickered at something. "Because I'm gonna have to go to the bathroom and get something to eat, and I have that timed to exactly the length of a standard basic cable commercial break. It's taken years of practice to do. If I deviate from the schedule I might have to go back and work my way up to it again. That could take years." He smirked at me. "And personally, I find you fucking annoying."

That drew a lop-sided grin out of Lucas. "I suppose you have something equally asinine to do?" I asked him.

"All Lucas does is watch TV and smoke," Dave said. "What else is he gonna do with all that free time but sit around and think up plans for stuff that hasn't happened yet? Besides, his brain is like a spotlight with cockroaches crawling around in it. Bright, really sleazy, and when he uses it sometimes there's this weird burning smell."

"That's not me thinking," Lucas said. "That's my charisma."

34

Dave

Even before Pete got drafted into Satan's Army, people had been clearing out; him dying and taking the blame for everything didn't slow the flow at all. For a week and a half the dorm parking lots were full 24-7 with parents in mini-vans trying to pack their kids and all their crap back home before we got to them. The best part was when they posted armed guards with clipboards at every parking lot entrance and exit, as though we might suddenly go stark raving mad and start attacking people in heavily-traveled well-lit areas, or in broad daylight. They did crap like that, and then they wondered why they couldn't catch us.

It was almost impossible to go anywhere in town. Between the mini-vans and unmarked police cars trying to pack us off to the Butt Rape Super 8, you couldn't get a Big Mac in under 30 minutes. Add the news trucks, the tourists, the combines and grain trucks on the roads because it was harvest season, and you could forget about doing anything quickly. Getting in a car and heading down to the liquor store used to take five minutes; now you had to plan it out and psyche yourself up for it like high school gym class. They started running human interest stories on the TV news about how bad the traffic situation was.

Lucas told me we were going to lay low indefinitely. The evacuation had slowed since Pete had moonwalked off this mortal coil, but anybody caught on the street after dark was being hauled in and questioned. This was bad for us, for obvious reasons--the most obvious being that I spent half of my time on the streets after dark covered with somebody else's blood. Also I think he was a little wary about Rachel hanging around. She'd proved she could kill somebody if we baby-walked her through it, but if we had to do that every time it was not only going to take all the fun out of it, it would mean that we weren't paying attention to other things.

The three of us had learned what to do as we went along, with Lucas leading the way and pointing out ways that we could do things more efficiently. He knew way more than me and Pete about everything it involved, and he'd taken the time to explain things to us and suggest ways that we could improve. There's more to it than busting down a door and stabbing some bitch in the tits. You have to have a certain finesse, an ability to adapt and improvise.

We'd done it so often that I took it for granted, so when Lucas said we had to show her the ropes, I didn't know what the hell he was talking about. He spent every night with her for two weeks, no less than two hours a night, conducting his own little murder academy. They went through *Gray's Anatomy* like Jesus freaks on a bible bender. He taught her about door locks--how to pick them, how to break them, how a simple inside chain-lock is almost impossible for someone to work in a panic. He taught her that if there were more than two locks on a door, you always left the even-numbered ones unlocked, because somebody on the run would almost always start trying them all in both directions, thereby locking some even while they were unlocking others.

He explained things like the psychology of fear and what to do when you were outnumbered. How to find other tools on short notice if there weren't any knives handy, and what to do with them. He told her about what we could take and what you had to leave behind, the ways to not draw attention to yourself when you were leaving the scene of the crime and the cop cars were already on their way.

I have to admit, I was a little shocked at how patient he was with her. Lucas is not known for his social graces or helpful attitude, and he can't stand to be questioned about anything. That chick, for her part, was lapping it up. I kept expecting to wander into his room and find her blowing him.

According to Lucas, who seemed to know everything about anything, the only worry we had was if the FBI was officially brought in. That couldn't happen unless we crossed state lines and killed somebody in a way that would directly link it to the ones we'd done so far. There was always the possibility that the cops would make something like that up--say they thought we crossed into Iowa and gutted some farm girl in her in a hayloft or something--but Lucas wasn't losing any sleep over it.

Then again, he never slept enough to have any to spare.

But that chick wasn't the only one who had to go to school--Lucas made me do it, too. He said that eventually the cops would find out where Pete hung out and with who, and that they would probably pick us up for questioning and maybe even search the house. The first thing we did was clean the place from top to bottom, starting with Pete's room. Lucas made that chick help, which I thought was hilarious, but he made me do the bathrooms, which wasn't amusing no matter how you looked at it. We took out every personal item of Pete's--clothes, pictures, anything that had his name on it--burned it in the grill in the backyard, and tossed the ashes in a dumpster in the next town over. We got rid of every beer bottle, cigarette butt, and food package that Pete had ever touched. Then we scrubbed everything with ammonia and hot water, from the handle on the front door to the Super Nintendo controllers in his old room.

When the house was Pete-free and thoroughly inspected, we started trashing it again. Not as bad as before, but just sort of messed up, to make the place look like bums like us actually lived there. We even spilled beer on the carpet and burned a couple of hamburgers to get rid of that nasty clean smell.

After all that, Lucas spent three nights straight with me, telling me how to conduct myself in a police interview. What to say, what not to say. We had been seen with Pete a lot, especially in his dorm when we were over there scamming stuff, so we knew they would find us before long. He told me a bunch of different tricks they'd use to try to scare me or trip me up, and what to do about it. The whole thing took the respect I had for him and cranked it up a notch. Say what you will about him, Lucas is fucking *sharp*. That guy doesn't miss a trick.

The last thing he told me was the best. "They don't have shit," he said. "If they did, we'd be locked up already. They've already got their guy, they're just gonna be fishing.

Don't bite, and pretty soon they'll pack it up and go home."

"Are you sure?" Rachel said.

"They want it to be over," Lucas told us. "They've looked like a bunch of assholes for too long to want to drag it out anymore."

"Is it over?" I said.

He just looked at me and grinned.

35

Dave

Brushing your teeth is important, and I take it seriously. The American Dental Association says that to maintain good oral health you should brush at least twice a day, floss regularly, and use some sort of fluoride rinse no less than three times a week, in addition to visiting the dentist of your choice twice a year for an examination and thorough cleaning. That's all well and good, if you can afford about two thousand bucks a year for some guy to poke around in your mouth with sharp crap, try to make banal conversation with you while he's got his rubber-gloved fingers in your mouth, and make you spit in a sink about a hundred times to get rid of that sandy tutti-frutti toothpaste he uses. Me, I just like to do some serious brushing. I brush after meals, after cigarettes, when I wake up, before I go to bed, and any other time my mouth is feeling not-so-fresh, because who the hell wants a mouth that feels and smells like a sewer?

So I was brushing my teeth for the second time in ten minutes, because the first time didn't take the way I wanted it to, when that chick came grunting up the stairs from the basement holding her stomach.

"Too many beers?" I said. I was kicking through the piles of books and papers on our living room floor, trying to find the art assignment I may or may not have done. We were supposed to sketch a bowl of fruit with charcoal. Jesus Christ. Like I keep fruit around the house. I remembered doing some sketches of a really slutty chick with saggy tits shoving a rotten banana in her twat and butthole while somebody took a big dirty crap in her mouth, because that seemed more amusing to me, and I think that at some point I had actually done the stupid bowl-of-produce thing, but I didn't know where I had put it. I might have just gotten drunk and imagined the whole thing, for all I know. A bowl of rotten apples and pears was rolling around in my head somewhere, and I'm pretty sure that I'd actually put it on paper at some point.

"I only had three," the chick said.

"Good for you," I said, because she took so long to answer I'd already forgotten what I'd asked her. Then I remembered. "You're gonna puke off three beers? What a wuss."

She flipped me off, then spazzed out and ran into the bathroom with her hand clapped over her mouth. Which was nice, considering I had a mouthful of toothpaste and the sink was in there. I spit it into her backpack on the couch and zipped it up, then rinsed my mouth out in the kitchen sink. Lucas came up the stairs, looked at the closed bathroom door, which wasn't doing anything to muffle the violent retching sounds Strawberry Slutcake was making in there.

Lucas was looking pretty bad. To steal one of his own phrases, he looked like he'd been ridden hard and put away wet. Of course, he'd just gotten out of the shower, so that might have had something to do with it.

"Sunshine!" I said. "What dragged your pretty face out of bed so early?"

"Test."

If Lucas harbors any hopes of being chosen as the Great Communicator of his generation, I hope for his sake that the debates are at night. Mornings are definitely not his peak hours, unless he's been up all night and comes at them through the back door. "What class?" I said. "Uses of the Word *'The?'* Literature of the French Menstrual Period?"

He took a can of warm Mountain Dew out of the mangled box beside the trashcan and started swallowing a handful of vitamins, one at a time. Somebody had picked up all the used paper towels and wrappers off the floor and changed the trash bag. I know I didn't do it. I'm pretty sure Lucas didn't do it, although if it got done it was usually him. Pete was worm-food. So unless we had been blessed in the night with anal-retentive elves, that left She-Ra, Princess of Puking, who was still trying to see what her intestines looked like, from the sound of it.

"What's wrong with her?" he said between vitamin C tablets.

"Beats me," I shrugged. "I barely even talked to her."

Slutbow Brite flushed the crapper and staggered out of

the bathroom, wiping her mouth on a wad of the brown paper towels we were using for shit tickets. "Everything come out okay?" I said.

"Fuck off."

"You two should settle down and start a family," I said. "A whole clan of grouchy bastards. You can all sit around the breakfast table and hope somebody chokes on a Pop-Tart."

Lucas kept swallowing pills; the chick turned on the tap in the kitchen sink and looked around for a clean glass before deciding to just cup her hand and drink from it like a monkey. Chicks in the morning = not fucking sexy at all, I'm telling you. I was just waiting for her to cock one hip to the side and rip ass, which would have completed the image nicely.

"Is he always like this?" she said between juicy slurps.

"No." Lucas said. "Usually his hair is dirtier."

That hurt. Well, not really. In fact, it had no effect on me at all. I only said that because I'm a liar, but I'm also a quitter, so it all evens out in the end, if you think about it.

"If you keep making jokes about me being dirty, I'm gonna get a complex," I said.

"You could get a shower instead," Teen Whore Barbie said.

"Bite me. How come you're here, anyway? Don't you have a house or a cardboard box or something to go to?"

She looked at Lucas, but he had stopped taking vitamins and started sifting through his dope bag for something pretty to swallow. "I kind of fell asleep in Lucas' room," she mumbled.

I backhanded Luke in the arm and grinned.

"Shut the fuck up," he said.

"I didn't sleep with him, you pervert," she said. She was green around the gills and beginning to turn a lovely shade of gray without any Revlon warpaint to cover it up. "I was on the floor."

"Sure, whatever you say," I smiled charmingly.

"Get your mind out of the gutter, you--"

And then she was off to the races again with her hand clamped over her mouth, only this time she forgot to shut the bathroom door behind her, so we were treated to the visual aspects of her hurking her guts out instead of having to settle for the radio version.

"It's always nice to be told you have your mind in the gutter by a girl who stops to puke in mid-sentence," I said.

One of Lucas' eyebrows raised as she groaned and let loose with another Technicolor yawn. This time she did rip ass, and I'm not talking about one of those little poots that chicks will do when they're trying to slip one by you in a noisy room, either. It was a full-on truck driver special that sounded like the cheeks of her ass were applauding themselves. I am not exaggerating in the slightest when I say that I found it completely appalling. Seriously. I mean, Jesus. I don't even like to think about chicks farting, let alone hear it. Especially when it sounds like a fat man.

"She didn't drink that much," Lucas said, which I thought was a very strange place to make that particular observation.

"She spent the night sleeping next to you," I offered. "That'd make me heave when I woke up." She retched again. "Man, she's gonna chip the toilet."

"Three beers never did that to anybody." Lucas lit a cigarette and watched her try to wipe a chunky string of drool off her chin. I say "try" because she mostly just rubbed it in and got it all over her hand.

"Well, except Pete," I said. "But he was only three apples high." Slutopatra staggered out of the bathroom and fell into the wall. "You okay?" I asked.

Her eyes rolled back in her head. "I think I'm gonna die."

"Heh. You and every other chick who's ever spent the night with Lucas," I said, which I thought was fairly amusing. Lucas wasn't impressed. By the time I got to the word "Lucas" she'd already fainted anyway, so who gives a fuck what she thought?

36

Dave

So then we had to haul her over to the hospital, which I found surprising, because I wasn't even sure Friedman had a hospital and I had no idea where it was. Lucas drove straight to it, another step toward proving my theory that he has way too much information rolling around in his head. Seriously, I've never seen that guy get lost, not one time. If I didn't know better I'd swear he has the ability to learn by osmosis and uses a different reference book for a pillow every night.

Rachel told them whatever her problem was and they put her in some exam room and told us to have a seat in these big turquoise chairs. I guess the place wasn't all that bad as far as cleanliness goes, but I'd only been in hospitals around Chicago. Compared to those, that place was a dump. I'm not saying that the Chicago hospitals look good, mind you, but at least they pay somebody a lot of money to make them look like shit. This place had checkered tile floors like a grade school and all the walls were painted the color of old vanilla pudding. And all they had to read were old issues of *Sports Illustrated* from like five years ago and some *Time* and *Newsweek,* so we flipped through those and watched people walk back and forth trying to look busy while dressed in those garish, ugly fucking nurses' uniforms that make them look like lunch ladies at clown school. Boring. And if there's one thing I hate, it's being forced to be bored on somebody else's behalf.

"This is disgusting," I said, and threw my issue of *Sports Illustrated* with Bo Jackson on the over onto the nearest table. "They don't have any good magazines, and the ones they do have are all scummy. You know what people do when they come here? Sit around and cry and snot it up, then they wipe their noses with their hands and keep turning pages. I bet these things have germs penicillin is afraid of."

Lucas looked at me and kept reading. That asshole.

"What the fuck is taking so long?" I said.

"Go get a doughnut."

"Not unless it's free," I said.

And he gave me some money, because he's like the dad I

always wanted when it comes to that. He's the only person who's never bitched about giving me stuff all the time, which is strange when you consider the fact that he's hands-down the most unfriendly person I've ever met. Not that that's a bad thing, necessarily. When you think about it, if you just stop somewhere and look around you, who the hell is worth being friendly to anymore? Chicks all tell you they're a bitch, like that's supposed to really impress you, like you're gonna have any sort of respect for them. Guys all want everyone to think they're a son of a bitch, I guess because then you won't be as inclined to mess with them. But the thing is, if you do mess with them, they're just a candy-ass like everybody else. Candy-asses that talk loud and walk around with their chests out and their arms hanging all stiff at their sides, like they're getting ready to ask you which way the gym is. It's pretty pathetic.

And pardon my rosy-red ass for getting a little philosophical here, but everybody's got it all wrong. I had it wrong too, until I met Lucas. Because Lucas is a son of a bitch right down to the bone. He doesn't talk loud--he barely talks at all--and he sure doesn't swagger around trying to convince you in advance that he can kick the living shit out of you if you cross him. Yeah, he'll kill somebody and not think twice about it. But he'll take a chick we barely know to the hospital and sit around for hours in a shitty, boring waiting room when he should be taking a test. He'll give my bitch-ass money for a doughnut while we're there. He's a son of a bitch, but he's a real one. He does whatever occurs to him to do, he helps you out if you need it, and he never asks for anything in return. And that's what makes it work. He doesn't need you, he doesn't need anybody. He knows it and you know it. And he never brings it up, because he also knows that to not bring it up is to make sure that you always remember it.

37

<u>Rachel</u>

Being deep in cold water, with your lungs about to burst from holding your breath longer than you knew you could, kicking and kicking and kicking, flailing your arms to get to the surface and the sunlight, then your head breaking through to air, late-August hot, the humidity thick enough to choke you, gasping in that hot air, your head confused and reeling at the temperature change, your lungs revolting at the nastiness of the oxygen you're finally giving them, your brain a filthy, flushing toilet behind the grainy, dry feeling of your eyes and the tight, drawn sensation of water evaporating off your face so fast it feels like your skin is shrinking. That's what it felt like when they told me. That same feeling, the worst of it, over and over again every 30 seconds. The sound of butcher paper crackling under my panty-clad butt, the hem of the paper gown tickle-kissing the tops of my knees, my feet numb and sleepy in my socks, goosebumps on my back where the gown gapped.

They asked me if anyone had come in with me and I told them Lucas. I didn't think about it. I had forgotten about Dave; when they left to get Lucas and I remembered, I was glad he hadn't crossed my mind. I didn't want him in there with me. I just didn't.

Lucas gave me a quick once-over and turned his eyes to the glass-fronted cabinets, the black bulb, cuff and hose of the blood pressure device mounted on the wall. His eyes ran over everything in the room with unhurried sweeps, avoiding me, taking in everything else, and I wondered what he would steal, if he had the opportunity. What could he find a use for?

"Where's Dave?" I asked, because we were alone, and somebody had to say something.

"Getting something to eat."

Coupled with the antiseptic smell of the examination room, the silence between us was like death. He stood there, hands in the pockets of his jeans, and didn't look at me. Waiting.

"Pregnant," I said.

He looked at me, just for an instant and then away again, his eyelids easing down in a lazy, natural blink while his pupils made a gentle U-shape and found their way back to his inventory. I loved him for that. Not passionate, poetry love--needy love. I needed him. Someone whose eyes weren't going to dart away and make me feel dirty and ashamed and cheap.

"Aren't you going to say anything?" I asked.

"No."

"Good." I threw both arms around him and squeezed, burying my face in the scent of his hair and clean skin and the dryer-sheet warmth of the flannel on his shoulder. He didn't hug me back, didn't take his hands out of his pockets, and I didn't care. I let go of him and sat back with my hands folded in my lap, trying to sniff my tears back. "Pretty stupid, huh?" I smiled.

The doctor came in with a clipboard and his stethoscope draped around his neck like a thin rubber stole. His light brown hair was beginning to gray at the temples and it looked good on him. "Morning," he said to Lucas. "You're the father?"

"Yes," I said quickly. The idea that this doctor, who'd I'd only met an hour before, could think that I was the kind of white trash whore who got knocked up by one guy and was already making time with another was too much to take. Lucas looked at me, his face not giving away anything to anybody, and remained silent.

"Good," the doctor said. He sat down at the writing desk bolted to the wall under one of the cabinets and made his hands busy with a prescription pad. "He should hear this. The reason you've had such bad morning sickness and this fainting spell is that your iron is low. You've probably had some bad headaches and generally felt tired, right?"

I nodded. "Is that bad?"

"Not good, but it's not uncommon," the doctor said. "I'll give you a prescription for some iron tablets, two pills three times a day. Start taking them today. And make an appointment to see your obstetrician."

My obstetrician. As if I did this all the time. "Will it be okay?" I said.

"Catching it this early, I'm sure you won't have any

problems. Your OB/GYN will do another check-up and then you'll know for sure. In the meantime I wouldn't worry about it. Just be sure you eat balanced meals and get plenty of rest." He began writing out the order for the iron tablets as I got dressed. "Any questions, dad?"

Lucas looked at me, saw I was almost naked and looked away, quickly this time. "No."

The doctor handed him the slip and grinned. "Congratulations."

I glanced up just in time to catch his one-sided smirk. "Thanks."

Dave was wandering up and down the hallway with a cup of hot chocolate and a jelly doughnut, peeking into rooms while he stuffed his face. "So?" he said.

Lucas already had an unlit cigarette in his fingers, working some strange acrobatic trick with it that had been done so often it was effortless. "Pregnant."

"You devil," Dave grinned. "Works that quick, huh?"

"Shut the fuck up."

38

Rachel

Dave was slouched down and half-sprawled in the tiny backseat of Lucas' Camaro, tapping out a soft punk rock beat with his fingers on the cover of his sketch book. "What time is it?"

Lucas tossed a spent butt out the window and looked at the digital clock on the stereo face. It read 3:41. "Almost eleven."

"Fuck. Can you drop me off? I think I have a test."

Lucas cranked the tape deck, so we were treated to W.A.S.P. screaming "Fuck Like A Beast" and "I Wanna Be Somebody" between the hospital and the campus. We stopped on the back side of the Heating Plant Annex, where most of the three-dimensional art classes were held; I leaned up so Dave could crawl out of the car. We waited until he was at the door and turned around with his mouth open in a fake scream, pointing at us like an arena full of rabid metal fans, before Lucas put the car in gear again and we moved.

"Is he playing with a full deck?" I asked.

One corner of Lucas' mouth went up. "Are any of us?"

"I guess not. But it seems like he might only have two cards," I said. I knew which cards, too--the Joker and the Ace of Spades.

We eased to a stop at the intersection. "You hungry?" he said.

"Sure."

He took me to a diner that I vaguely remembered seeing on a corner of the square but had never been in. The door met the sidewalk at an odd angle and it was much bigger inside than it looked from the street. The whole place seemed to be brown and cream colored, with low lighting and yellow pebbled glass dividers between the booths. We got a booth toward the front window, in the smoking section, and ordered. It was just before the lunch rush. Every time somebody pushed through the swinging kitchen door we could hear Lou Reed's *Transformer* album playing on a boom box the Mexican staff were using to pass the time.

I watched Lucas light a cigarette. Before he put the pack back in his shirt pocket he tilted it toward me.

"I guess not," I said.

He tucked the pack away and looked at me. "Well?"

"I don't know." My fingernails were suddenly very interesting. More appealing than looking him in the eye, anyway. "I know who the father is, if that's what you mean. He's gonna be a little hard to reach."

Lucas nodded and looked out the window, sucking in smoke and breathing it out again. His sunglasses were perched just above his hairline and I watched his eyes follow someone or something I couldn't see on the street, filing the details away.

"No offense," I smiled, "but you really need to work on your conversational skills."

He blew another stream of smoke. "Then I'd have to talk all the time."

"That would be a shame."

He shrugged. "Lot of bother."

Communicating with other human beings as a "lot of bother" wasn't an idea I'd ever considered. Thank God. "Have you always been this quiet?" I said. "And if so, why, for chrissakes?"

"Don't have anything to say."

"Yeah, right." The waitress brought our plates and asked if we needed anything else. We didn't. Lucas examined his plate and pushed it away, sliding the ashtray closer to him instead.

I smeared two French fries through a glob of ketchup and stuffed them into my mouth. As the one who didn't consider communication to be "a lot of bother," it was up to me to create and then direct some sort of conversation. I hate to eat in silence. Especially if I'm sitting with somebody. "There's no way I'm giving it up for adoption. I guess that only leaves two options."

"You can't get ahold of the dad?"

"You took care of that for me about six weeks ago," I said, trying to cross-reference *ahold* in my tiny database of regional dialects. I liked the sound of it, but it wasn't something I heard often. "He picked me up at a party and we did it. It wasn't date rape, but it was close. He probably wouldn't give a shit if he was around to tell."

I leaned forward and lowered my voice, checking around for any possible eavesdroppers. "Big white house, four guys and two girls. Do you remember? He had this scummy Grateful Dead hair with blonde streaks in it. Total dirty-hippie sheik."

I was hoping for all the bloody details with an extra helping of gore. It almost felt as though I was entitled, if that makes any sense. Lucas' mouth pulled back slightly at the corners and he lit another cigarette.

"I know, I know," I said. "Everybody has one horror story, right?"

"Not that bad."

I flipped him the bird. There was a thin line of ketchup on my fingernail. "Screw," I said.

"That's what got you into trouble in the first place."

"You're really a smug prick," I said. "You know that?"

"You're the one who wanted conversation."

"If this qualifies as conversation, I pity you."

"You know what I pity?" he said, and gave me one of those irritating one-sided grins. "A Dead '72 bootleg for mood music and a tye-dyed condom."

"That's not how it was," I said. "He didn't use a condom."

"How lovely for you."

"And it was a live Phish album," I muttered. It was starting to seem funny, for some reason.

"What'd he do when it was over? Offer you the Ben and Jerry's Phish Food or the Cherry Garcia?"

I gave him a look that I hoped would cut glass. "Would you shut up?"

39

Rachel

It's always uncomfortable when people you've recently met and find that you like come to the place you live for the first time. There's this maddening urge to impress them somehow, to prove to them that your place and your things are interesting without seeming to brag. You want to show them everything so you show them nothing and hope that by chance they will notice something, ask about it and thereby get the ball rolling. If they do see something and show any sort of interest in it, you play it down like it's no big deal, like it's so old-hat to you that you can't believe anybody would get excited about it, even though the reality of the situation is, if it hadn't excited you at some point, you wouldn't have bought or collected it in the first place.

People as a whole are such fakers.

My apartment was what you would describe on the housing spectrum as upper-middle slum. The walls were a bland cream color, the furniture consisted of a couch and chair upholstered in a beige-and-powder blue material that had given over to the gritty texture my brothers called "sock turds" long before I ever signed the lease, and a cheap coffee- and end-table set made of pressboard, scarred through the plastic wood-grain finish in several places that revealed the yellow crap beneath. The carpet was a standard shit-brown semi-shag, the lamps were big and ugly and didn't match each other or anything else. Basically it was a lot like Lucas and Dave's house, only cleaner. A lot cleaner.

Being the narcissistic bastards that they are, the only thing in my apartment that really interested them was the collage of press clippings about the murders that I'd put up over the television set. Well, Dave was interested. Lucas seemed as though he was only looking at them to be polite. I put on The Donnas *Get Skintight* CD and turned the volume to a level that wouldn't discourage conversation, if anybody felt like making any.

"What do you think?" I asked.

"Man," Dave said. "I thought we had depraved hobbies."

"I wanted to ask you guys something," I said. "You were doing people every few days, but then you didn't do anymore for almost a month."

Lucas didn't look at me. Dave waited for a few seconds. "I didn't hear a question in any of that."

"Well, how come?"

Dave picked up my pack of cigarettes on the coffee table, smelled it, shook one out and smelled that, then stuck it back in the pack and took another one out to smoke. "Oh yeah! That first week *The Wonder Years* marathon was on. After that, we have no excuse. We're just lazy. Actually we watched it like three more times, because I taped it." He took the cigarette out of his mouth, looked at it as if it tasted strange, and turned to Lucas. "It's surprising how the hotness of Winnie Cooper distracts one from mindless bloodshed."

"Becky Slater, all the way," Lucas said.

"Yeah, she beat the crap out of Kevin every other episode," Dave nodded. "I need a chick like that. A girlfriend who'll beat me like a red-assed monkey at least once a week."

"I think it should be more frequent than that," Lucas said.

"Yeah," I added, "and it doesn't necessarily have to be your girlfriend."

He whirled on me, shouting "You want to fight me don't you? Don't you?"

I gave him my best smug smile. "You're digging your own grave, Meyer."

"Holy shit!" he hooted. "A chick who makes *Better Off Dead* references! Marry me. I'll treat you like shit and make you fix me hamburgers at 4:00 in the morning. You'll love it."

"Sounds thrilling, but no."

"Not good enough for me, huh?" he said. "Better you realize it now than later, I guess."

"I just don't want you taking half my money when they hear my story in Hollywood and want to make a movie out of it."

Dave's eyebrows took a dive toward the bridge of his nose. "You know what? When we get caught, and they make a made-for-TV movie about us, our parents still won't be proud." He looked at the cigarette again. "Well, my mom might. She really likes those movies. And I know for sure my grandma would. Grandmas are proud no matter what. You could be a crack dealer and your grandma would still be proud of you."

"So you think dealing crack is worse, morally, than killing people?" I asked.

"Serial killers need to have some degree of intelligence and ambition," he said, as if it were so obvious it was pathetic that he had to point it out to me at all. "Crack dealers just make phone calls and have sex and sleep all day."

"So the sex and phone calls make them inferior?" I smiled.

There was a pregnant pause.

"Yes. Back to the movie of the week, who do you want to play you?"

"Meredith Baxter-Birney," Lucas said.

Dave snorted laughter so hard he almost swallowed his cigarette. "He didn't say your mom," I told him. "He said you."

Lucas stared at me. "Meredith Baxter-Birney."

"My mom would be played by Rosie O'Donnell," Dave said, "because *Newsweek* says she's the Queen of Nice."

"That was *Time*," I told him. I vaguely remembered reading that sycophantic piece of shit article somewhere.

"Was it?" Dave asked.

Lucas shrugged.

"Anyway, I don't care who plays me, because I plan on coming back from hell to possess whoever they get. But my girlfriend has to be played by Sabrina, or Clarissa, or whoever that hot blonde girl is."

"You don't have a girlfriend," I said.

"Yeah, but movies need sex. Like with no clothes on. And somebody has to cry over me and pretend like they give a crap."

"They don't really show naked girls on TV," I said.

"Fuck, I didn't think about that."

"And," Lucas offered, "Clarissa's image is too wholesome for her real talents to be exposed."

"God-fucking-damn it," Dave said. "Well in that case, maybe they could get Becky Slater. She needs work."

"She still won't be naked," Lucas told him.

Dave sighed. "I hate my life."

I grabbed an ashtray from the end able and swung it under Dave's hand in time to catch the two-inch piece of ash that was getting ready to fall on my carpet. "Hey," I said, "do you guys know that Becky and Winnie are sisters in real life?"

"Yes," they said.

It wasn't until we were already in my apartment that I realized there was absolutely nothing to do there. The weather was decent if you had a sweatshirt, so we decided to walk to the movies and see whichever one looked the worst. Dave and Lucas went out to smoke on the sidewalk while they waited for me to use the little girls' room and brush my teeth.

It only took me ten minutes or so, but that was enough. When I opened the door to my apartment, two uniformed cops were frisking them against the side of a police car. Dave was giggling.

"Do you have any weapons or drug paraphernalia on your person?" one of the officers asked. "If so, tell me now. If I find them on my own, we're gonna have a problem."

"There's a grenade up my ass," Dave told him. "I don't mind if you try to get it out, just like, you know, don't pull the pin by accident or anything."

Another cruiser pulled into the lot and the cop gave Dave a shove that sent his nose into the trunk. "You think this is a joke? Do you think I'm playing with you, sir?"

"Which question should I answer first?" Dave grinned.

"Hey, what's going on?" I called down.

The cops looked at me. "You know these two?" the second cop said.

I glanced at Lucas and he nodded with his eyes. "Yeah," I said. "We're getting ready to go to the movies. What did they do?"

The second cop climbed the stairs and flipped out his

notepad. "Your name, please?"

I gave it to him. "I live in this apartment," I said, pointing to the open door. "What's going on?"

The other two cops cuffed Lucas and stuck him in the back of the first car, murmuring to each other over the squawk of the radios on their shoulders.

The second cop, who was older and had a blonde mustache that was beginning to go gray, climbed the steps to my apartment. "Ma'am, we got a report of two suspicious gentlemen loitering in front of the complex. When we stopped to investigate and called them in, we found out that they're wanted for questioning."

"About what?" I said.

"I'm not allowed to comment on that," he said. "Could you tell me how long you've known these two?"

I pretended to think about it, but what I was really thinking about was if Dave and Lucas had given their real names. "About a month," I said, and pointed to Lucas in the second car. "He was helping me with a term paper, and then we just sort of started hanging out."

"What about the other one?"

"Just as long," I nodded. People were starting to wander out of their apartments onto the decks by then, chattering into cell phones. In other apartments the doors stayed closed, but the curtains in the front windows were being pulled aside for not-so-sneaky peeks. "They're roommates."

"What about their other roommate?" the cop said. "Peter Bilotti. Did you know him as well?"

I frowned. "What?   They don't have any other

roommates." I chewed my bottom lip in a fashion I hoped was charming. "That name sounds familiar, though."

The cop stole a look at my tits and I knew I was on the right path. "And while you were with them, you never met a Peter or a Pete?"

"No."

"Did you ever hear them mention anyone by that name?"

"I don't think so," I shrugged. "Who is he?"

"Ma'am, we may need to ask you a few more questions at a later time. If so, would you be willing to come down to the police station for an interview?"

"Sure," I said, and gave him my phone number. He flipped his book shut. "What's all this about?" I asked.

"It's probably nothing," he smiled. That same lying dog's smile I'd seen my stepdad give a thousand times. "The station says bring 'em in, so we bring 'em in. Thanks for your help."

"No trouble," I said. "I hope everything's okay."

"I'm sure it is," he said.

At least one of us was sure. Dave was grinning at me through the window of the squad car as they pulled away, and I wasn't sure of anything at all. People were angling toward me with hopeful smiles on their faces, hoping I would give them some dirt they could pass around to their friends. Those fucking scumbags. I'd lived in that apartment for more than two months, and until that point none of them could even be bothered to return a wave. Now they all wanted to be buddies.

I turned my back on all of them and locked the apartment

door behind me.

40

Dave

They stuck me in a room with a table and three chairs and gave me a can of Mountain Dew. It was piss-warm, but I drank it anyway, because who am I to not take advantage of free anything? I waited around for like an hour before anybody came in to talk to me, which was what Lucas told me to expect. Apparently the idea is that if you leave a scumbag in a room by himself with no windows and a warm soda for a while, he'll freak out and confess to something. I don't know how this replaced bright lights, a rubber hose and being handcuffed to a radiator, but they might need to rethink that.

After an hour, I really had to pee. Bad. I was starting to think about filling the can up again with some good old Mountain Dave when some big asshole threw the door open and started staring me down. He was maybe the size of Lucas, if you went by the stats, but he didn't look as big. And he sure didn't look as mean.

"Who put this piece of shit in here?" he yelled at somebody in the hallway. "He should be in a holding cell."

"I hope the holding cell has a urinal in it," I told him. "Cause if it doesn't, you might want to put me in the janitor closet with the mops to save time."

He grabbed me by the back of my t-shirt and tossed me out into the hall. I dropped the can, but picked it up, cause

I'm polite. "Here you go, sir," I told him. "It's empty. I don't want a littering ticket."

"Oh you're a fucking cutie-pie, aren't you?" he said, but I could tell he didn't mean it.

"You seem like a nice guy, but I'm only into the ladies," I told him, and held the can out. He slapped it out of my hand, which made me laugh. A couple of drops came out and landed on the floor.

"I thought you said it was empty?" he growled.

I shrugged. "It's like taking a piss," I said. "No matter how long you shake it off, there's always a couple of drops left, right?"

No sense of humor whatsoever, that guy. He bounced me off the walls all the way to the holding cell, which made a couple of uniformed cops who were just standing around laugh and egg him on. Then he opened the door and kicked me in the ass for good measure, just in case I wasn't sure where I was supposed to go.

"I can't wait to get a crack at you," he said. He grinned at me like I should be scared of him.

"I think you just got my crack," I said, and rubbed my ass. "I hope you're not religious. Cause if you decide to get holy on me, I don't have any lube."

He didn't have anything to say to that, I guess. He slammed the door, locked it, and punched the glass one time, which made me laugh some more. I almost expected him to start barking and spray spit all over it.

Lucky for both me and the custodial staff, the holding cell had a toilet and nobody else in it, so I could drain my lizard without stage fright. It didn't occur to me until I'd zipped up again that there was probably a camera in there somewhere watching everything I did. I took a seat on the steel bench bolted into the wall and waited. There wasn't even any graffiti in there to read, those censoring cocksuckers. To me, nasty graffiti always seemed like it might be the best part of going to jail. I mean, where else are you gonna read good stuff like that? The misspellings and grammatical errors alone would have been a riot.

I wondered where Luke was and what they were doing to him. Somehow I doubted they were bouncing him off walls and kicking him in the ass. Then again, they might have been. The only way they could have ever been considered bright was if you doused them with gas, set them on fire, and then put them out with a bucket of day-glo paint.

I waited around in the holding cell for awhile, maybe another half-hour or so. Then some other guy who had his hair all slicked back and stiff unlocked the door and motioned for me to come with him. I didn't get up.

"Are you gonna kick me in the ass like that other guy?" I said.

"What?" he said. He gave me one of the worst fake looks of surprise I've ever seen. "Who kicked you?"

"That other guy," I said. "The one who looks like a refrigerator with a tie stuck on it."

He pretended to be holding in some anger over that. I hope he wasn't an undercover guy. He couldn't act his way out of a grade school Christmas play. On the other hand, his feet looked smaller than the Fridge's, so if I was going to get booted again, it probably wouldn't cover as much area.

"I'm Lieutenant Reisman," he said, and held a hand out for me to shake. I shook with him, a real shake and not some weird elaborate one. It kind of threw me off for a minute. "I want to apologize if someone kicked you, David. That's not the way we do things here, and I'll get to the bottom of it."

I held up my hands like he'd just threatened to shoot me. "Hey, I don't want any problems," I said. Lucas had told me to fuck around a little bit, back off, and then fuck around some more. According to him it would show a healthy, normal fear of the police and give them the message that I didn't having anything particular to be nervous about.

We went into a room lined with file cabinets and sat down at a table, me across from Reisman and the Fridge. A guy with a stenography machine sat back from the table and off to the side, taking down everything we said.

"Do you know why you're here, David?" Reisman asked me. "Has anybody talked to you yet?"

"Nobody said anything," I told him. "I assumed it was because I know Pete Bilotti."

"That's right. We want to talk about your relationship with him. Could you tell us something about that?"

Lucas had prepared me for this, that lovable scamp. "I've known him since like, grade school," I said. "I think we met playing pee-wee soccer, but it might have been before that. We were seven, or eight maybe?"

"Good. Go on."

"We were best friends for a long time, through junior high and high school and all that. We came down here to go to school together, but after freshman year, we kind of didn't hang out together so much anymore."

Reisman wrote this down, which seemed a little redundant, considering that they were paying a guy to type everything we said. I guess typing pussies need to make a living too.

"Uh-huh," he said. "And why did you start drifting apart?"

I scratched the stubble on my cheek and paused like I was thinking of a good way to put it. "He kind of... well, he sort of turned into an asshole."

"Could you clarify 'asshole' for me?"

"I mean like a jerk. Sorry. Am I not supposed to swear?"

"Just give it to us as it comes to you," Reisman grinned. "We're all adults here." He tapped his pen on the table. "So how was he an 'asshole,' exactly?"

"He used to be a cool guy to hang out with," I said. "And he was still kind of cool, but then it seemed like he was always pissed off about something."

"Any idea what that might have been, or what triggered it?"

"Sure," I said. "He broke up with his girlfriend cause he found out she was cheating on him back home. She was a year behind us in school. And we found out that while he was down here, racking up huge phone bills and paying to bring her down for weekends and stuff, she was doing a bunch of guys up there."

"Really," Reisman said. He tried to play it cool, but he and the Fridge gave each other a not-so-secret look. "That would put anybody in a foul mood, huh?"

"Yeah," I said. "It got pretty nasty. We found out she got knocked up and had an abortion and everything. The whole deal was fucked up. He really treated her good, too."

"I see. And Pete, he had trouble getting over this?"

"I don't think he ever did," I told them. "I mean, you know, he was talking about getting married and stuff after they were finished with school. So that sucked. I figured he had a right to be pissed off, but after a couple of months, he still didn't get over it."

"Did he ever talk about other girls?" Reisman asked. "Girls he was interested in, girls he might have gotten some action off of here and there?"

I almost swallowed my tongue. *Gotten some action off of.* Jesus Christ. At least the guy didn't ask me if Pete like to chase skirts. Then I really would have lost it.

"Oh God no," I laughed. "That guy had zero chick skills after all that. I thought maybe he'd find another girlfriend or something, cause I mean, you know, there's all kinds of hot chicks down here who are way better than *that* fucking whore. I mean, you know, he always seemed like he was really into the whole process of having a girlfriend. Picking them up after work, buying them little shit for no reason, taking them out to dinner, the whole deal. A lot of guys just do it to get laid regular, you know? But he really liked the whole relationship thing. At least until it blew up in his face, I mean."

The best part of all this was that it was absolutely true. No shit. Petey the Pirate had been so in love with that girl, it

219

was disgusting to look at. And she did turn out to be a fucking whore, abortions and all. Last time we heard, she'd had three of them. In like, a year and a half. You think after three, the doctor would stop vacuuming them out of her and just sew her twat shut. But what do I know? Boats and country club memberships don't come cheap. He probably enjoyed the repeat business.

"How would you assess his attitudes toward women in general after this?" Reisman said. "I mean, was it just her, or did he sort of put the blame on all of them?"

"Oh yeah," I nodded. "All of them. He even said his mom was a no-good fucking cunt."

This was also true. But, to be fair, I knew Pete's mom. She *was* a no-good fucking cunt. She got a divorce from his dad the summer before our freshman year of high school, and her lawyers just tore that guy up. I mean, he got jack-fucking-squat, and still had to pay alimony, which was a joke, because her parents were fucking loaded and gave her money all the time anyway. It wasn't like she needed it. She just wanted to be a cunt. She's good at it, too.

At least she can do something well. She can't cook for shit.

That left Pete at home with two sisters and a man-hating mom, which is never a good thing. Especially when you look like your dad. She never beat him with a rake or anything, but it was always some pain in the ass, every time I went over there. It was always worth the trip, though. His mom hated my guts, which is entertaining under any circumstances, and his sisters both had huge fucking tits and a lot of hot slutty friends hanging around.

"Did he ever talk about hurting women, maybe getting revenge on them?" Reisman said.

I frowned. "Nah, I don't think so. I mean, he might have, but I can't really remember him doing it. We made a lot of jokes about chicks, but nothing seriously sick. We're guys, you know?"

Reisman looked at me. The Fridge was trying to stare holes in my face. "Just guys," Reisman said. "How would you describe your own relationships with women, David? Could we get into that a little bit?"

"I would say they're not that great," I told him, and he got a hungry look on his face. "I mean, I'm supposed to be totally honest with you, right?"

"Absolutely. Whatever you say in here stays between us."

Yeah. Us, and the typing guy, and everybody who reads what the typing guy typed. Just our cozy little inner circle. That fucking douchebag. Lucas had been right--if I got caught in a lie by this stupid piece of shit, I deserved to be put in a cell with a guy named Horsecock.

"I don't have a girlfriend or anything," I said. "And I'm not really into the whole bar scene or anything like that."

"You get much action?" Reisman asked. "Get a piece now and then?"

"I couldn't get laid in a morgue," I told him, and we all laughed, even the Fridge. But the joke was on them, since for me, the morgue is kind of like sloppy seconds.

"Why not?" Reisman said, still finding it funny. "I mean, you're a good-looking guy. What's the problem?"

I looked around the room. "Well... you know... I was raised Catholic. It sounds kind of stupid these days, but you know, the church says you should wait until you get married. And I'm not ready to get married."

Finally the Fridge piped up. "Good little alter boy, huh? You follow everything the Bible says, huh?"

"No way," I said. "I don't even believe in all of it. A lot of that stuff is just fucked up, stuff against gays and women and all that. I don't even go to services anymore, unless I'm back home. It keeps my parents off my back." I laughed and ran a hand through my hair. "I don't go down here. I'm not even sure where the Catholic church is."

"Cut the shit," the Fridge growled. "We know all about you, my man. You're not fooling anybody. Your friend Pete had help. A lot of it. And so far, we can't find anybody who would give that piece of shit the time of day except you and your big ugly friend."

"What?" I said. "You think I had something to do with all that? No way! Fuck no! I'd never do something like that!"

It threw a scare into me, I have to admit. Without Lucas warning me that they might do it, it would have scared me a whole lot worse. "If they start getting to you, just use it," he'd told me. "They'll expect you to be nervous. It's suspicious if you aren't. And they'll try to tell you that I already confessed, or that I ratted you out. They'll try anything. It's all bullshit. Stick to your story and don't get fancy with it, and you'll be alright."

The Fridge was getting right up in my face now, breathing his pig breath all over me. "You see all these file cabinets?" he said, pointing around the room. "They're full of you. We've got everything you've ever done. Now why we would do that, if you were innocent?"

I scooted back. "Maybe because you're a fucking idiot," I told him. "An idiot who needs a Tic-Tac. I didn't do shit. I don't know anything about Pete or anybody else killing anybody."

The Fridge looked like he was ready to belt me one. "We've got the files, shithead. And the files don't lie."

I looked at Reisman, but he wasn't going to be any help. Good-cop bad-cop was some shit that only happened on TV, or so I thought. It might be. TV is probably the only place in the world you can actually find a good cop.

"I didn't do shit," I told them.

"Files don't lie."

I thought about spitting in the Fridge's face, but that might have been taking it a little too far. And my mouth was dry. "You're probably right. But the kind of asshole who would bounce me off the walls and kick me into a cell would probably lie through his fucking teeth."

The cops looked at each other. "I want to see the files," I said. "I want to see what you made up about me."

Another look. They didn't have shit. "You're not allowed to see those, David," Reisman said. "It could compromise our investigation."

The Fridge opened his mouth to say something else, but I started screaming and banging my fists on the table. "That fucking asshole! I tried to be his friend and then he does this? And then gets me blamed for it? Fucking bullshit!

That no good piece of shit motherfucker!"

I jumped up out of my chair so fast it tipped over. "You tell me why you think I did that," I said. "I wanna know right now. Cause if you really think I killed any of those chicks, I want a lawyer. I've seen this stuff on TV. You're not gonna railroad me into jail, no fucking way."

"No one's trying to railroad you, David," Reisman said. "We just want to know what happened. We want to hear your side of the story."

"I was going to the fucking movies!" I screamed. "And then you handcuff me in front of a bunch of people and bring me in here, and this big fucking asshole starts shoving me around and kicking me, and then you tell me you think *I* did something wrong? Fuck you! I want a lawyer."

"Sit down," the Fridge said. "Lower your voice and sit down."

"You fucking sit down!" I told him. "Get away from me, you fucking gorilla. I didn't do anything! You're not supposed to treat people like this if they didn't do anything!"

"Son of a bitch," the Fridge said to Reisman. "He's almost as much trouble as the other one."

Reisman gave him a dirty look, and the Fridge shut up quick. "Why don't you tell us what you know about Tim Carpenter, David?" Reisman said.

It wasn't hard to look confused, because I had no idea who that guy was. "I never heard of him," I said. "What, he was supposed to be in on it too?"

"Tim Carpenter was a police officer," Reisman said. "He

was killed in the line of duty after we found your friend."

"That cop that got killed at K-Mart?" I said. I was trying to get my breath back.

"So you do know him."

"I know a cop got killed at K-Mart," I said. "It was in the paper. What's that got to do with Pete? He was already dead when that happened, right?"

"Yeah," the Fridge said. "But his best buddy in the whole world wasn't dead, was he?"

"I wasn't his best buddy in the whole world," I said, pretending like I was forcing myself to calm down. "Don't say that. I don't even want people knowing that I knew him, that sick fucker."

"You got a dirty mouth on you, kid," the Fridge told me.

"Yeah, but I got a clean conscience," I said. "How about you?"

"I sleep like a baby."

"Really? You shit your pants in the middle of the night?" I grinned, and he looked like he was gonna hit me again.

Reisman cleared his throat and rolled his pen in his fingers. "We've got surveillance tape of the Wal-Mart parking lot on the night Tim Carpenter was killed," he said.

I frowned. "What difference does that make, if somebody killed him at K-Mart?"

"It wasn't at K-Mart, David, it was at Wal-Mart, which I think you already know. That whole lot is monitored with state of the art security cameras. I bet you didn't know that, either."

He had me there. I *didn't* know that. I hoped Lucas did, or we were seriously fucked. "Okay, so they've got cameras at Wal-Mart," I shrugged. "What's that got to do with me?"

Reisman laid his pen down, smoothed his tie against his stomach, and put his palms on the table. "You killed Officer Tim Carpenter, David. And we have you on tape."

Holy lola. That'll put a hitch in your get-along, as I've heard Lucas say. If any of it had been true, I would have cracked like an egg right there. But since I actually *didn't* kill that cop, for once I was in the clear. And they were totally full of shit.

"I want to see it," I said. "I want to see this imaginary tape of me killing a cop."

The cops looked at each other again. Something was fouled up somewhere, that was for sure. I kept beating it. "Come on, right now. Either show me this magical tape you have of me killing somebody, or let me go home."

"It's in the evidence locker," Reisman said. "The officer with the keys to that locker is out for the evening."

Sweet shit. How fucking stupid did they think I was, that I would believe they only had one set of keys to anything? I'd always assumed we got away with everything because we we're just really good, but that theory was going straight down the crapper. These fucking buttholes couldn't catch crabs on uncle's night at a whorehouse.

I tipped my chair back up and sat down. "Okay," I said. "Okay. Can I ask you some questions?"

"I don't think--"

"I'm not trying to pretend like I know everything, but none of this makes any sense. There's no way I could have done that."

Reisman smiled like he knew something I didn't, which at that point I highly fucking doubted. "Oh, this should be good."

I was on shaky ground here, and I knew it. Lucas never said anything about Wal-Mart at all. "Do you know how far K-Mart is from my house?" I said.

"It was Wal-Mart."

"Same difference," I said. "In fact, Wal-Mart's even farther from my house. That's like, *miles.*"

"So?"

"So how is it you think I got there, exactly?" I said. "I don't have a car. I don't have a driver's license. I don't even have a fucking bicycle."

"Maybe you walked."

"Maybe you're out of your mind," I said. "Why would I walk miles, to Wal-Mart, to perform some incredible ninja skills, which I don't have, and shoot some cop, with a gun, which I also don't have?"

"He wasn't shot," Reisman frowned. "He was stabbed and beaten."

I snorted. "Do I look like the kind of guy who could stab and beat up a cop? You're out of your mind. I've never been in a fight in my life. I can't even run up stairs without having to take a nap."

"Looks can be deceiving," the Fridge said.

So can total bullshit, but not for very long. "If it was me, how did I get away, on foot, without anybody seeing me?"

"Maybe you got a ride with your friend," the Fridge said.

"I *know* that big ugly bastard's got a car. We ran the plates."

"So you have him on tape too, then."

They looked at each other again. Just a quick glance between assholes, but it was a look.

"We're not sure," Reisman said. "We're not done analyzing it yet."

It was incredible. Just total bullshit. "What else have you got on there?" I said. "Unicorns? Oompa-Loompas? Bigfoot with a wristwatch walking through the background?"

"We're getting off the subject here," Reisman said, and smoothed down his nice paisley tie, even though it wasn't wrinkled.

I leaned my chair back on two legs. "The subject being you trying to get me to admit to something I didn't do, or you just trying to frame me?"

The Fridge started moving in my direction, and I don't think he wanted to give my face a grandma-wash with some spit and Kleenex. "You've got an answer for everything, don't you?" he said.

"At least somebody does," I told him. "You two don't seem to have an answer for anything, unless you make it up and stick me in the middle of it."

Reisman turned to the stenographer guy and smiled. "It's getting nasty in here, isn't it?" he said. "I think we're gonna take a ten minute break and give everybody a chance to cool off. That okay with you?"

The typing pussy smiled back. "Sure, I'll just step out grab a cup of coffee. Anybody else want anything?"

"Mountain Dew," I said, and he gave me a dirty look

before he shut the door behind him.

As soon as the door clicked, the Fridge kicked the two back legs of the chair out from under me. Dropped me right on my fucking head, that ape. As far as head injuries go, I've had better, but it was still pretty good.

"Now," he grinned. "Where were we?"

Reisman tapped his pen on his notepad and smiled. "I think David was just about to cut the shit and start being straight with us. Weren't you, David?"

The Fridge hauled me back into the chair by my hair and wiped his hand on his slacks. "Jesus Christ, you're a fucking dirtbag."

"I hope you know how to run a sour cream gun," I told him. "Cause when I get out of here, I'm gonna scream police brutality, and you're gonna be arresting refried beans at Taco Bell, you fucking pig."

The Fridge was so pissed off, he couldn't even talk. Unfortunately for me, he could still hit me with his forearms, which seemed like a weird choice until Lucas told me later that it probably didn't leave any marks, or at least marks that didn't look like a fist. He did that a few times in my ribs and back, grazed my balls with his knee, and was choking that shit out of me with the collar of my own t-shirt when the typing guy came back. Without my Mountain Dew, that pansy cocksucker.

"Rhodes is here," he said. "He's got that Dawson woman with him."

Reisman had a look on his face like he'd just swallowed something large and hot that didn't agree with him at all.

"What's he doing?"

The typing pussy smirked. "Right now they're staring at that gorilla in the holding cell," he said. "What's the matter Frenchie, you losing your touch? The guy looks like he's thinking about taking a Sunday nap in there."

Frenchie the Fridge grunted. "Don't even get me started on that fucking guy. He takes a shot like a goddamn sandbag."

They didn't have shit. I knew it. And if Frenchie the Fridge had been thumping on Lucas, he was gonna get defrosted in a bad, bad way. They kept me in there for about another hour, asking me questions over and over again, but they got nothing. Frenchie the Fridge even roughed me up a little more, especially when I just kept grinning at him. How could I not? It was like somebody wanting you to be afraid of your dead grandma.

I couldn't have wiped the grin off my face with a razorblade.

41

Dave

Lucas was already in the holding cell, sitting on the bench and watching the window like he might have been asleep with his eyes open. I took a seat next to him. "So, how's it going?" I said. "You been gettin' any?"

One side of his mouth went up. "Every now and again," he said. "How 'bout your own bad self?"

"Oh, fuck yeah," I said. "I been getting a lot of *action*.

More ass than a toilet seat, you wanna know the truth."

Lucas grinned at me. Through his teeth, quietly, he said "They're prolly taping us now."

I nodded. "You know that cop they said got killed at K-Mart?" I asked him, in a normal voice. "They were asking me about that. They tried to tell me they had me on video doing it and everything, those fucking assholes. Then when I told them I wanted to see it, they said they didn't have the key to the room where it's locked up."

"That's weird," Lucas said. He yawned and looked at me. "You think they'd have more than one set of keys to something like that."

"Yeah," I said. This was actually turning out to be sort of fun, now that we were together again. "Did they smack you around at all? Cause they thumped on me pretty good."

Lucas looked at me to see if I was kidding, and I nodded. "You okay?"

"My ribs hurt, and the back of my head, and my balls," I told him. "I'm not gonna die or anything. That sucks, though. I didn't think cops really did shit like that."

"They're not supposed to," Lucas grinned, and I could tell that big brain of his was already working on something. There was no clock we could see, but we sat in there talking about our usual stupid crap and making each other laugh for a long time. Every once in a while somebody would come by and look in the window to make sure we weren't killing each other or getting romantic or anything. "We're totally gonna miss *The Wonder Years* every time it's on today, you know that don't you?" I said.

"Who cares?" he shrugged. "We've got a bunch of them on tape."

"True," I said. "But somehow it's just not the same. Plus, I have to take a dump, but I don't really want to do that in front of you."

"I appreciate that."

"I thought you might."

"I can turn the other way," he said, "but I don't have enough hands to plug my nose and ears at the same time."

"Yeah, and I don't have any burning desire to see myself on some scat website either," I told him.

"I guess that makes you shit out of luck then, don't it?" he grinned, and started cracking his knuckles. "How's your balls?"

"Better. I don't think I'm gonna feel like touching them for a while, though."

"Thank God for small favors."

"Fuck you, small favors," I said. "You couldn't carry my nuts in a wheelbarrow."

"There's a disappointment. I had one all picked out and everything."

"You probably did, you homo."

"I did," he nodded. "It was a nice one, too. The whole thing was lined with fake pink fur and there were black leather tassels on the handles."

I scooted away from him. "What did they do, give you Sodium Fagathol or something?"

He gave me one of those irritating one-sided grins of his. "Don't you know how this works?" he said. "In prison, the guy who gets fucked is the queer one. The guy who does the fucking is just doing what he has to do."

"What?" I said. "No fucking way. You're making that up."

"Nope. Learned it in Sociology last year."

"I don't care where you learned it, it's horseshit. And how does being raped by another dude make you the gay one? That's like somebody stealing your bicycle and then having you arrested for being a thief."

A uniformed cop opened the door and opened his mouth to say something, but there were more pressing matters at hand. "Hey," I said, "can I ask you something?"

The cop's eyebrows went up. "What?"

"We're having an argument here, and I think this guy is full of shit. Is it true that if a guy gets butt-raped in prison, they consider him the gay one, and not the guy who fucked him?"

The cop laughed. Hard. "I hadn't heard that one. I don't know. Why, you worried about something?"

"It's bad enough somebody would hold you down and fuck you in the butt," I told him. "That's just wrong to begin with. But then to call you a queer on top of that... that's just ridiculous."

"It sounds fishy to me," he said. "It's not gonna matter to you tonight, anyway. You guys are going home."

I managed not to jump for joy as we followed him out of the cell, but it was tough. They took us into the interrogation room, handed us trays full of our stuff and made us go through it and sign a receipt so we couldn't come back later and say that they stole something from us, I guess. The first thing we did was put our belts back on, because that whole walking-around-while-you-hold-up-your-pants routine was getting old. We put everything back in our pockets and had started re-lacing our shoes when my new best friend Lieutenant Reisman came back to pay us another visit.

He looked bad. Like one-step-from-a-stroke bad. "It looks like you guys are off the hook for now," he said.

"That's good," I told him. "Since we never should have been on the fucking hook in the first place."

That didn't help his disposition any. "Yeah? Well I'm gonna be keeping an eye on you, smartass. Cause to me, you're dirty. And if you so much as *look* like you're about to do anything I don't like, you're gonna be right back in here with me and my partner, and we're gonna take up right where we left off. You understand me?"

I grinned at him. It's always so much easier to grin at a fucking asshole when you've got Lucas right beside you, you know it? "That reminds me," I said. "Have you got one of those police brutality forms I can fill out? I might as well go ahead and do that while I'm here."

"You might as well get the fuck out of here while you still can," Reisman snarled, and left.

I looked at Lucas, who was grinning to himself about something while he finished tying his boots. "Did you know that before he became a cop, he used to perform at children's parties?" I said.

"Nope."

"Yeah, he had a whole routine," I said. We stood up and

walked out into the hall. "He would make balloon animals, which all looked like snakes. And if the kids didn't say that it looked like a giraffe, he'd beat them with a phone book."

42

Rachel

After hours of me waiting around, having one panic attack after another and wondering if I should go out and try to kill a few people on my own to take the heat off of them, Dave and Lucas showed up at my apartment. Dave was walking like a stiff old man, but Lucas didn't look any different than usual, except for the little one-sided grin on his face.

"Well?" I said.

"How's it going there?" Dave said. "I'm gonna use your bathroom, if you don't mind."

I looked at Lucas. "What's wrong with him? Why is he walking like that?"

"They roughed him up a little bit," Lucas said. "He'll be alright."

"What about you?" I smiled. "They didn't try to rough you up?"

That one-sided grin got a little bigger and he lit a cigarette. "Anything good happen while we were gone?"

I told him how I'd been thinking about going out on my own, since they were already locked up and had an airtight alibi. "I just couldn't do it, though," I said. "I was afraid I'd screw it up."

He nodded. Whether this was because he understood my fear or because he also thought I would screw it up, I don't know. Either way, the subject seemed to be closed, which was good enough for me.

"So come on, cough it up," I told him, and dropped down beside him on the couch. "They let you out, so it can't be all bad."

"We're still under suspicion," Lucas smirked. "They think we did something, but they don't have anything to back it up."

"Hey!" Dave called through the bathroom wall. "Stop talking."

"Why?" I called back.

The toilet flushed, and the sink ran, and a can of air freshener sounded like he was trying to empty it. Then he came out, closing the bathroom door behind him. "Sorry about that," he said, and held out his hand. Lucas threw him a cigarette. "I never took a crap at a chick's house before," he frowned. "It kind of makes you feel weird."

There was no way I wanted to get into that particular conversation. "Why did you tell us to stop talking?" I said.

"Because I didn't want to miss anything, and that big asshole never says anything twice," Dave said. He flopped down in my chair and propped his feet up on the coffeetable with a wince.

"What's the matter with you?" I said.

"I got my ass kicked," he said, and told me all about it. When he was finished he raided my fridge and came back with a Mountain Dew. "Now," he said, settling back in the chair with a smaller wince, "what I want to know is, what the fuck were they talking about? Do they really have cameras in that parking lot, or what?"

Lucas nodded. "They were broken that night. That whole week, actually."

Dave grinned. "You went to Wal-Mart and broke their cameras? No way."

"Already broken. I heard some girl talking about it," Lucas said. "She's the assistant manager or some bullshit. She said they'd been broken for a week, and it was gonna be another week before the technician came in to fix them."

I personally found this appalling. Who just overhears something like that, files it away for future reference, and then actually puts it to use the way he had? That's beyond crafty--it's fucking diabolical.

"And where did you hear this, exactly?" I asked.

"Some class."

This was only slightly more enlightening, since I had no idea what classes Lucas was enrolled in. When I had asked Dave at some point, he'd shrugged and asked me who gave a fuck. "I've seen the papers he has to write," he said. "His classes are even more fucking boring than mine are, and mine are enough to make you want to put a gun in your mouth."

"Was she hot?" Dave said. "The Wal-Mart chick?"

Lucas moved his mouth without actually making it do anything and stubbed out his butt. "Not particularly."

Dave grinned. "What kind of not particularly, in particular?"

Lucas seemed to give the question about 3.4 seconds of intense thought. "Hyphenated?"

"Yeah."

"The I-still-live-with-my-parents-but-I'm-working-my-way-through-school-because-I-like-to-pretend-I'm-independent kind of not particularly," Lucas said. "And the I-have-shitty-high-school-hair-and-a-redneck-boyfriend-with-an-agricultural-manual-labor-job-and-I-wear-white-low-top-off-brand-athletic-shoes-with-thick-colored-socks kind."

"Ugh," Dave said. "Alright, I'm convinced."

"It never ceases to amaze me how charming you two are," I said, and they both gave me the finger.

"Are you sure those things were broken?" Dave said. "Because they sounded pretty sure of themselves. At least, you know, as far as two dicksmacks like that could."

Lucas' one-sided smile made a triumphant return. A few more of those, and his face would probably explode. "Did they say anything to you about her being there?"

Her meaning me, of course. Come to think of it, I'm not sure I ever heard him say my name.

Dave thought about it and frowned. "No. They said they had me on tape, and then when I was asking them why they thought I would walk miles to kill somebody, they kind of freaked out a little bit and told me that you were on there, too." He thought some more and shook his head. "They never mentioned her once."

"What does that mean?" I said.

"It's means they've got jack-fucking-squat," Lucas told us.

"Because if they did, they'd know it was her that got him first, and she would have been right in there with us."

"Son-of-a-bitch!" Dave hooted. "Man, is that good news. I was really started to get freaked out for a little bit."

"Hey," I said. "Do you even know what my name is?"

Lucas looked at me. And since I was already looking at him, there was no question about who I was talking to.

"Yes, you," I said. "I have a name, you know."

All I really wanted was to hear him say it. I think he might have, too.

"I don't think you like the name you have," Dave said, "so it doesn't really make any difference anyway."

"What's wrong with my name?" I said.

"I didn't say there was anything wrong with it, I just said you don't like it. I think you want to change it."

"Oh, this should be brilliant," I said. "And just what would I like to change it to, exactly?"

Dave gave me one of those smug fucking grins that make me want to rip his face off and feed it to him. "Mrs. Lucas," he said.

What are you supposed to say to something like that? I glanced at Lucas, who looked like he was putting a maximum effort into doing me the favor of not smiling.

Those fucking assholes.

To Be Continued in

The Gentle Art of

Making Enemies--

Volume II

Kevin Mellor lives in central Illinois and is a graduate of Western Illinois University. *The Gentle Art of Making Enemies* is his first novel.

www.ingramcontent.com/pod-product-compliance
Lightning Source LLC
Chambersburg PA
CBHW072227170626
46813CB00003B/1123